KING'S ROAD

A SAVAGE KINGS MC NOVEL AND PREQUEL TO CHASE

D.B. WEST

LANE HART

COPYRIGHT

Editor's Choice Publishing

P.O. Box 10024

Greensboro, NC 27404

Edited by: All About the Edits
Cover by: Marianne Nowicki of PremadeEbookCoverShop.com

FOREWORD

WARNING: THIS BOOK IS INTENDED FOR MATURE READERS ONLY BECAUSE IT CONTAINS ADULT LANGUAGE AND EXPLICIT SEX SCENES.

INTRODUCTION

King's Road is a prequel to Chase, the first book in the Savage Kings MC series. It can be read before or after Chase.

PROLOGUE

Chase Fury

2012

"Chase! What got you up so bright and early today?" Deacon asks as I close the door to the chapel behind me. He's in here by himself this morning, looking over our account books. His expression changes from a smile of greeting to a look of concern as he sees what I'm holding in my hands. "Today's the day then, is it?"

"Today's the day." I walk over to him and place my cut on the table, then pull the holster containing my pistol from my back and lay it on top of my leather. "Take good care of them now, treat them like your own," I add, before turning and starting to walk away.

"Chase, wait a second, hold your horses!" Deacon barks. I stop in my tracks at his tone, knowing this is the president of my MC giving me an order, not my uncle talking to his nephew. "You don't have to do this alone."

When he sees the scowl darken my face, he raises a hand to halt my outburst. He knows full well how bad my temper can be, and how sensitive I am about this particular subject. "You're a brother in the Savage Kings now. We honor our own and stand by them through anything. Every one of us knows the pain you've gone through, and we understand what you have to do. That bastard hurt you, he hurt you deep, and even though he's been in prison all this time and he's paid his 'debt to society'—"

"He hasn't paid his debt to *me*," I growl, my vision blurring as my blood pressure rises, rage pounding through every muscle and nerve.

"Do you even know where to find him?" Deacon asks pointedly. "Or are you going to tear Emerald Isle apart looking for him?"

"Reese has been in the prison's database. He had to list an address for his parole officer, so I know exactly where he's staying," I confirm.

"You can't just bust into his momma's house to confront him. Don't give him an excuse to shoot you. You've gotta get him out somewhere, not on his turf, you understand?"

"I'm not the starry-eyed prospect you need to lecture anymore, Deacon," I tell him, not unkindly. "I might have been a naïve little shit when I first signed on, but with everything that has happened I... I've changed."

"Yeah, you have, Chase. You've grown up. You're a damn fine brother, a true King amongst the Savages. More than that, you're a good man. Remember that, when you face him. You're a better man than he is. You've let your anger tear you apart every moment of every day since the accident, since Sasha..."

"Don't!" I roar. "Don't talk to me about her. That's mine to bear, no one else. I won't let anyone use her memory to try and influence me. Not even you, old man."

"Stop talking about her like she's dead, Chase," Deacon says quietly, standing up to come over and put his hand on my arm. "You have to remember that she did recover, and she's out there right now, living a good life. No matter what happened between you two, remember that."

"She recovered," I agree. "I didn't. You said I've become a good brother, a good King, but I don't feel that way. I feel like everything that was good about me died out there in that damn intersection, when an old drunk decided to go for a joy ride and ended up ripping her out of my life. Now, are you going to try and stop me, or can I go handle my business?"

"I would never try to stop you," Deacon says, wrapping me in a fierce hug. "If anything, I'm proud of you. No matter what happens, the club will be there to support you, even when your ass ends up in prison. We've got quite a bit of influence, even there. All I would ask is this: Don't kill him, unless you absolutely have to. Your family needs you, the *whole* you." Deacon pauses, rubbing at his eyes. "Hell, I wish Rubin was here to talk to you. He founded this club with me, and he was always better with advice. Just...just remember that you're the future of this club. Get better and get back to us."

"I can't promise that." I sigh as I hug him back. "Without her, I..." I trail off as my voice breaks. "Sometimes, the only thing that kept me going was dreaming of the day when I could finally face him. I hope she hears about this, I hope Sasha..."

"Hush, boy," Deacon whispers, hugging me tighter. "Don't ever start down that road. You're Chase Fury, and you're the closest thing I've ever had to a son of my own. Embrace your namesake, and never give in to despair. Now go. Show that bastard what it means to cross the Savage Kings. When you're done, I'll be here to hang this cut back on you personally."

With a final clap on the back, we break our embrace, neither of us willing to look each other in the eye and see the tears that might be threatening to fall. I turn and stomp out of the chapel, not even pausing when I hear Deacon break into a hacking cough behind me.

3

CHAPTER ONE

A few weeks later...

I glance over the top of the book I'm reading when one of the guards stops outside my cell. "This is you, Cross," he says, as one of the biggest sons-of-bitches I've ever seen in this place steps forward and casts a shadow over me.

I watch the sad-eyed giant warily as he takes his blanket roll over to the bunk across from me. Then I go ahead and get to my feet, just in case this guy has got some fool notion he needs to pick a fight to establish dominance.

I'm pleasantly surprised when, instead of doing anything crazy, he just sits down on the edge of his bed and sticks one of his ham hands out to me for a shake. "Hey, man," he says. "I'm Abe."

"Chase," I tell him, skipping his hand and grabbing his forearm in a brotherly clasp, the way my boys in the MC greet each other. The big man seems pretty laid-back, so I stand down and take a seat on the edge of my bed, facing him. "I guess you know the drill, Abe. We're gonna be cellmates, so what are you in for?"

"Stole a car." Abe sighs, looking out into the common room

where dozens of our fellow inmates are milling around aimlessly. "But what a fucking car, you should have seen her. It was a 1957 Jaguar XKSS. That's what fucked me, really. With my priors and the value of the damned thing, I took a plea and ended up getting eighteen months."

"That ain't bad, man, you must not have had any violent priors."

"Nah," Abe says, waving one of his massive paws dismissively. "I'm not proud of it, but I've had to scrape by stealing for a long time. When you're my size, thieving isn't really the best career choice, it turns out. So, what about you. What brings you to this fine establishment?"

I'm still grinning at the idea of this big idiot being a shoplifter or pickpocket. "Assault with a deadly weapon, inflicting serious bodily injury," I tell him, being completely upfront. You have to be honest in here when asked what you're charged with. These pricks find out you're trying to hide that you hurt kids or something, and they will fuck you up. "Got fourteen months for taking a crowbar and smashing a guys' kneecaps."

"You only got fourteen months for *that?*" Abe asks as he leans away from me, his face going a little pale. "What kind of fucking world do we live in where I'm serving more time for—"

"First offense," I interrupt him, knowing where his thoughts are going. "It isn't much time for what I did, but the MC I run with has a good lawyer. Hell, the truth is, the District Attorney and even the guy I assaulted all knew he had it coming." I realize my voice has dropped to almost a growl as I continue. "It shouldn't even have been called a fucking assault. It was justice. The only *real* justice in this miserable world. An eye for an eye, or a knee for a fucking knee."

I feel the rush of blood to my face and the pounding in my skull as my simmering rage explodes into a boil. It's been bubbling furiously in me ever since the night of the accident three years ago that cost me the only woman I've ever truly loved. When Abe came into the stuffy cell I was already lying on my bunk with my shirt off, but I suddenly feel like I'm about to burst into flames. I get up and go over to the sink in our cell to splash some cold water on my head and neck.

"I'm gonna have to do that to cool off too," Abe says as I grip the edges of the sink tightly. "It's hotter than hell in here. You said something about your MC has a good lawyer? That tattoo on your back, the 'Savage Kings,' is that your motorcycle club?"

"Yeah," I tell him, still trying to rein in my anger. I thought it would get easier after I confronted the drunk driver who hit me and destroyed my life. I thought that once he was released from prison, I would face him, smack him around a bit, and hear a sincere apology from a man who had changed his ways to get some sort of closure.

Instead, when I tracked the putrid little shit down the day he got out of prison, he cursed at me for getting in his face. He told me that while he regretted the accident, he had found solace in the fact that he 'only hit some biker punk and his junkie-whore girlfriend.' Just remembering the contempt on his face when he said those words to me makes me tremble in rage, the veins in my forearms bulging under the skin from my grip on the sink.

The only reason I'm not in jail for murder is that I had confronted him in public. We were outside of a bar down on the Sunset Strip, where plenty of witnesses could call the police when they saw a man smashing another man's kneecaps with a crowbar. By the time the police got there, I had beaten his legs until I could see the bones shifting under the skin, knocked out a handful of his teeth, and begun breaking each of his fingers, one slow crack at a time. That son-of-a-bitch is only alive because I wanted him to suffer for what he had done to her, and I wanted him to feel a fraction of the pain he had caused us...

"So, what about that tattoo on your chest?" Abe asks me, his voice floating through the red haze of rage my memories had evoked. "It says Sasha, right? Who is that, your...what do you guys call it, your 'old lady'?"

"I can't talk about her," I growl at him. "Don't ask me again."

"Oh shit, man, I know how that is," Abe replies. I've still got my back to him, so I can't see his face, but I can hear the surprise in his voice, and what sounds like...like he's laughing. "I've heard that getting a girl's name tattooed on you is the kiss of death for a relationship. You fall in love with the wrong girl, and find out she's a crackhead or a whore, then, next thing you know..."

"She's not some junkie whore!" I scream at him as I spin around, my right fist crashing down on the side of Abe's face. His skin splits open, splatters of blood flying across the cell as his head rocks sideways. All I can see is the blood, my senses overwhelmed by the memory of her, the smell of burnt rubber and charred skin, and her blood on my hands. "She was everything to me! Everything!"

The strange screeching of my own voice brings me back to my senses, my fist cocked again, ready to crush the man who destroyed me. Instead of a middle-aged drunk, though, I see a wounded giant sprawled across his cot, his hands raised to try to ward me off.

"Chase, shit, oh shit, man! I didn't know. I didn't mean to set you off. I won't ask about her, all right? Peace, brother. H-how about we start over?" Abe asks as I back away, panting, desperately trying to clear my head from the flashbacks that sweep over me.

"Well, look at this. Fury is already giving the new meat a warm welcome," a voice says from outside our cell. Abe pushes himself back to a sitting position, then stands up as a tall, lean man with a swastika tattoo taking up most of his chest steps in with us. He's got two other men with him who take up positions just outside, their arms crossed.

"What the fuck do you want, Randy?" I snarl, still trying to get myself under control.

"Just came by to check out our new recruit here, and extend an invitation to this fine specimen," Randy says as he turns to Abe. "A man needs someone watching his back in this place, and our brotherhood is always ready to welcome one of our brethren. What's your name, boy?"

"Abe Cross," he replies warily. He's much bigger than our uninvited guest, but after he misspoke to me a moment ago and got

8

punched, he seems to be more cautious about what he says, and to whom.

"Well, Abe Cross, the Aryan Brotherhood could use a man of your obvious gifts on our side," Randy tells Abe, before I abruptly interrupt.

"Get out of my goddamned cell, Randy. We don't need to hear your sales pitch because we aren't buying what you're selling," I tell him.

"Now, Fury, just because you turned us down doesn't mean that the new meat here might not want our kind of protection. Hell, he might need it from you, from what I can see," Randy says, dragging a hand across his clean-shaven scalp. "What do you think, Abe Cross?"

"I'm not a racist," Abe replies simply, shrugging his shoulders.

All three of the skinheads burst into laughter at that, turning to smile at each other. "You hear this poor boy?" Randy tells his companions. "He says he's not a racist. Let me tell you something, Abe Cross," Randy continues, his voice dropping almost to a purr. "It doesn't matter if you're a racist or not. Because all those boys gathered out there..." Randy waves an arm over the common room, taking in all the gathered prisoners. "All those boys you see, black, yellow, white, or green are all plenty racist *for you*. You can cry yourself to sleep at night after one of those gangs beats you half to death, consoling yourself in the knowledge that at least *you* weren't a racist, like them. Is that what you want, boy? Or do you want someone watching your back while you're here?"

"He'll have someone watching his back," I say, pushing past Abe to get right up in Randy's face. "You know damned well not to try your bullshit anywhere near me. You're not recruiting my damned cellmate, now piss off."

"Randy," one of the skinheads outside our cell calls out in warning as another group of men approaches.

Randy turns to take a look at the half-dozen black men who stop just outside, then throws up his hands in surrender as he steps out of my cell.

"Yo, Chase, everything all right in there?" one of the men asks.

"Thanks for stopping by, T.J.," I call out to my friend.

"These peckerwoods bothering you?" He points at the three skin-heads standing only a few feet away.

"We were just leaving," Randy says. "But maybe we'll talk again later, Fury. Keep in mind what I said, Cross," he calls back as they finally head back out into the common area.

I wave T.J. over and he steps into the cell while his boys spread out outside, casually leaning against the bars. "T.J., this is my new cellmate, Abe Cross. Abe, this is T.J. He's a member of an MC that has a relationship with my club."

Abe takes a moment to get a wad of toilet paper, which he holds up to the bleeding bruise on the side of his face, then reaches out to shake T.J.'s hand. "Nice to meet you," he says. "Now, can I ask what the hell is going on here? Chase, I'm sorry about what I said a minute ago, I won't bring it up again, but...man, what is all this?"

"This is prison, son," T.J. answers with a laugh. "Boy, look at you, all puppy breath and baby butt cheeks. Don't see many this smooth and fresh in here anymore."

"I wasn't much different when I arrived," I remind T.J., getting another laugh out of him.

"That's true, your ass would have had a purely unpleasant time if you didn't have such sterling and upstanding friends in the commu-nity. Sit down, big man, and let me tell you all about how this works." T.J. motions to Abe. "So, let's start simple," he begins as he leans casually against my bunk. "I'm a founding member of the Outer Banks O.G.'s MC. You ever heard of us?"

"No," Abe says, almost apologetically. "But I've never heard of his Savage Kings MC either," he adds, pointing at me.

"That's nothing to be ashamed of, man, you just run in different circles, that's all," T.J. says dismissively. "Now, the MC I'm with has a variety of enterprises up and down the East Coast. The Savage Kings MC has some infrastructure that helps support our businesses. You understanding this?"

"Yeah." Abe nods. "You get the Savage Kings' help moving shit around."

"That's it exactly! Moving shit around, that makes it sound nice," T.J. replies with a smile. "Now, since we have a long-standing relationship of trust and fellowship, when certain members of our organizations find themselves indisposed in the prison system, we've reached mutually beneficial agreements to assist each other. You still following?"

"He's just saying that my MC called in some favors and paid some folks to watch my back while I'm here," I interrupt. "And to keep those meth-head fucking Aryans out of my hair. We've had to bloody them up a few times to keep them out of our neighborhood."

"Well, that explains what just happened here," Abe says with a frown. "But it doesn't do me much good. You think those guys are going to keep fucking with me?"

"No," I tell Abe firmly. "I meant what I said. You're my cellmate, and if you're sleeping next to me, I want to trust you. That means I've got your back in here, and by extension, so do my friends."

"Well, now, about that," T.J. says. "That might require some sweetening of the deal..."

I just grin, then stick out my hand to clasp forearms with T.J. "How about I get a little extra in the deliveries the next few weeks, keep you and your boys in that good grass you love?"

"That is why I love you, boy, you know just how many lumps I like in my coffee. You white boys grow the best damned weed I've had since I got back from Colorado. You make that happen, and your big friend can sleep in the arms of angels, just like you."

"Deal," I agree. "I'll make the call tonight, and get it arranged. I appreciate you, man," I tell him sincerely.

"We appreciate your business, as well, my man. Keep an eye to your backside, though. Those peckerwoods ain't gonna be happy to be denied a prize like that," T.J. adds, pointing to Abe before stepping out of our cell and rounding up his crew.

"Chase, man...thanks," Abe says, still holding the wad of toilet paper to his jaw.

"I owed you one for snapping like that," I reply. "I shouldn't have done that, I just...I get a little crazy when I think of her. We're going to be locked in here together with nothing to do for a while. It will be a lot easier if we can trust each other."

"I feel better already knowing you and those friends of yours," Abe admits. "I was scared shitless coming into this place. Everyone must be able to tell just looking at me, that I've never been to 'real' prison before."

"We're locked up in here with hundreds of predators, man, some greater than others. Hell yeah, they can sense that shit, like blood in the water. I'll show you how to ride straight and true, brother. You just stick close, all right?"

"Sounds like a plan," Abe agrees, wincing as he peels the wad of toilet paper off of his face.

"You all right, man, you need to see the nurse or something?" I ask him.

"Nah, I've had worse lumps on my head than this. I used to do some motorcycle 'repossessions' down in South Carolina and dropped a couple without a helmet. This is nothing, really." Abe chuckles.

"Legal repossessions, or just 'property transfers'?" I ask him with a grin.

"Both," Abe answers with a wink.

"So, you can ride, sounds like," I observe. "You ever think about joining a MC? Sounds like you already live the dream, like the guys I ride with, you just don't have a family to call your own."

"Ha! Living the dream, is that what you call this?" Abe snorts.

"You do things your own way, with all the risks and rewards that come with standing on your own. That's what my MC, my family, stands for. We live how we want and support each other, whatever comes. I think you might just fit in."

"I've got family," Abe says in a sad and subdued voice. "A

younger brother. I suppose that's why I never stayed in one place long enough to put down roots. Our mother was an addict, and we got put into foster care. We didn't get placed together, though. My brother, Gabriel, he's not..." Abe pauses, like he's trying to find the right words, before finally just waving a hand down the length of his body. "He's not like me. He's not scary. He got placed into a home pretty easy. I didn't, and ended up running away to follow him around, keep tabs on him. I'd take any work I could find to get money, to help support him, and that's how..."

"That's how you ultimately ended up here, huh?" I finish for him.

"Yeah, that's how I ended up here. Like you said, that's the life we chose. Big risks, big rewards. You really think...you really think your MC might talk to me?" Abe asks, staring at me hopefully.

"They're my family. If I bring a friend home and introduce him, they treat him like a guest. Now, if they offered you a chance to prospect, you might have a rough time, but once you're a full member—"

"Prospect?" Abe interrupts me. "What, like one of those gang-banger initiations?"

I snort and step over to the cell door, looking down at the common area below us. "Not quite," I explain. "Those street gangs usually require you to kill someone, show loyalty by shedding blood. That's not how we operate. Prospecting with the Savage Kings is a chance for all of the members to get to know you, and for you to see what we're about. You're held to all the same standards as a full member, and you get to use our facilities and come to all our events. What you don't get is a seat at the table, or a vote in any club-related issues. You're also expected to take orders from full members, but that's not really a huge deal. I mean, no one ever forces prospects to eat spiders or wear a dress all day."

"That's kind of vague," Abe observes. "I mean, you're a member, don't you have to do what you're told by guys that rank higher than you anyway?"

"Yeah, I do for now, but my patch is still fresh. I've only been with them a few years. As you gain more rank in the club, you become a shot-caller. Doesn't really matter though, members vote on everything, and all of our profits are split equally after club bills are paid. Even prospects get a percentage, and their own room in the clubhouse."

"What kind of people do you guys recruit? I mean, do you teach people how to ride a motorcycle if they want to join?"

I actually burst out laughing at that and turn to see Abe looking at me with a raised eyebrow, obviously a little confused. "No, man, we're a motorcycle club. We do have some standards, and being able to actually ride a bike..." I trail off, then flop back down onto my bunk. "I didn't mean to laugh at you, man, I was just thinking of this kid who showed up at the club all gung-ho to join and didn't know how to ride. Some of my brothers fucked with him for a while, before they sent him packing. There is some training while you prospect, but it's all about your responsibilities as a member. For us, teaching someone to ride would be like having to teach them to lace up their boots."

Before Abe can ask me any more questions, an alarm buzzes throughout the cell block, and prisoners begin filing by outside our door. "It's only about five o'clock," Abe observes. "We going outside or something?"

"Nah man, that's the dinner bell on D-block," I tell him as I pull my shirt over my head. "We get to bed early in this house. Come on."

With a nod, Abe gets up and falls into line behind me. After roll is called for the umpteenth time today, our entire block of inmates file down to the cafeteria. As we wait in line for our trays, I have to force myself to stop chewing on my lip nervously. Anxiety, not hunger, is gnawing at my stomach and after a moment, I glance back in line to check on my new cellmate.

"Hey, Abe, get in front of me in the line," I say.

"Yeah thanks, man. I'm starving," Abe agrees with a grin.

14

"Stay sharp," I mutter as he passes me. "Something feels odd in here."

Abe's eyebrows lower in a scowl, and he gives me a quick nod before picking up a plastic tray and turning to the food being passed out. I grab a tray, keeping my back to the servers as I try to figure out where to look in a room filled with possible threats.

It doesn't take me long to figure out what was triggering my apprehension. The Aryans are camped out at a table directly behind the line getting their food, and every one of them has their eyes on me. I see Randy's lips move just before three of his enforcers stand up and turn towards me.

I lean over to Abe and slap him gently on the arm. "Go get a seat and get out of the way. You don't want to get dragged into this."

"What?" Abe says, turning to follow my gaze as one of the three skinheads—a fat, bald man—steps forward.

"We've had enough of you and your apes telling us what to do, Fury," he says, as he slaps the plastic tray I'm holding to the floor. "You're going to..."

I never got to find out what I was going to do, because Abe slams his tray into the skinhead's face, spraying carrots and mashed potatoes everywhere. Abe lets out an ear-splitting roar, then his right leg shoots up in a Spartan kick to the fat man's gut, sending him sprawling into his buddy behind him. They both slip in the spilled food, crashing to the ground together. The third Aryan looks to his two friends incredulously, before rushing forward and slamming his shoulder into Abe, trying to tackle him to the ground.

I grab the back of the man's shirt, jerking him away from Abe, then kicked him in the back of the knee. He loses his balance and staggers back towards Abe, who immediately slams a huge fist into his chin, sending teeth and blood flying. Snatching him by the neck, Abe tosses him in a limp heap beside his two friends, who were still trying to get to their feet.

The alarm sounds as the rest of the Aryans' table leap to their feet. I move closer to Abe so that we could fight together, but then breathe a heavy sigh of relief as the four guards assigned to the cafeteria moved in with their batons drawn. Placing our hands on our heads, we moved back against the wall at their orders.

All of the other inmates in the cafeteria, including the Aryans and my allies in the Outer Banks OG's, who had been further back in the line, move to stand by the walls while the guards surround the men Abe had knocked down. The sergeant on duty, a broad-shouldered, burly woman, surveys the three Aryans who the other guards are restraining before casting a stern eye on me.

"What the hell happened here, Fury?" she demands.

Before I can even open my mouth, the inmate who had been serving the food pops up from where he had been hiding behind the stack of trays. "I'll tell you what happened, these fools have lost their goddamned minds! Look at this, look at this, Sergeant! There's blood in the mashed potatoes, and a goddamned tooth to boot!"

"Benny!" the sergeant barks at the wiry old man, as he slaps his serving spoon into the potatoes, which looks like they had been doused with a line of ketchup. "Get a grip on yourself. What exactly happened here, or to your potatoes?"

I see a hint of a smile on the sergeant's face as Benny bangs his spoon on the platter again before pointing it accusingly at the Aryans. "This whole damned place has gone crazy! Used to be black boys, white boys, and them Latino boys didn't like each other. Now I got to deal with these bald peckerwoods trying to attack big ol' hairy crackers like him! In my supper line, no less! It was them three right there, Sergeant, came strutting over here, proud as you please, and picked a fight with that fish right there." Benny points his spoon at Abe, before slamming it down once more on the serving platter, looking for all the world as if he had just adjourned the court. With a final nod, he snatches up the mashed potatoes and disappears back into the kitchen.

The sergeant casts a dubious gaze up at Abe, before turning back to me. "Is that the way of it, Fury? Those three try to shake down the fish?" she asks, using the same slang Benny had used, to refer to a new prisoner.

"More or less." I nod. "He's a big one, and they want him bald. From the looks of things, he doesn't share their worldview."

"All right." The sergeant gives me a subtle wink. "Get those three down to the SHU. A little solitary will give them time to recuperate," she orders the guards. "The rest of you get back in line and get your dinner. But if I even hear a dirty word from any one of you, I'll put your whole unit on lockdown, you hear me?"

Once Abe and I secure fresh trays, we wait for the OG's to pick a table, then sit down with their crew. We eat in silence, though I catch Abe glancing around nervously as other inmates walk by us.

Once I've scarfed down the tasteless mess on my plate, I wait for Abe to finish before breaking the silence. "You handled yourself well back there, man. Especially when you kicked that fat bastard. That was pretty badass."

"I've always wanted to do that ever since I saw that movie 300," Abe says with a grin. "Remember that scene, where the Spartan kicked that Persian into the big pit? I can't believe that worked."

"I've never watched all of that movie," I admit. "Wasn't it the one with all the naked fight scenes?"

"They weren't bare-ass naked," Abe scoffs. "It wasn't gay porn."

"Well, you have to admit that it was at least, how do you say it...homoerotic?"

"It was not!" Abe replies. "Trust me, my little brother Gabe made us watch the old *He-Man* cartoons growing up. You know the one, with Prince Adam, who wore the pink vest and tights? I never realized it when I was kid, but He-Man couldn't have been gayer if he shot rainbows out of his ass. Now *that* was homoerotic. 300 is just a masterpiece."

I snort and laugh, loud enough that the OG's turn to look at me and see if I was choking. "You all right?" T.J. asks from across the table.

"Yeah, man, just having too much fun tonight. My fruit cup was on point, and we even got a show with our dinner."

"Yeah, your new buddy can handle his business. Keep that one close and maybe my boys can relax a little." T.J. stares at me for a moment, searching my face. "I gotta say, man, it's good to see you laugh at something. You're all right, but you can be a grumpy mother-fucker, you know that?"

This time, Abe snorts and grins at me. I stand up and pat him on the shoulder before I reply. "I might have heard that a few times. Thanks for everything today. I'll make that call we discussed later. Come on, Abe, let's go line up and get out of here."

Once we get escorted back to our block, Abe and I head to our cell. "I didn't want to bring it up while we were out there with every-one," Abe says as we sat down on our respective bunks. "But it seemed like that guard didn't ask many questions and let me off pretty easy. I ain't mad now, but the way she acted made it seem like she knows you."

"She's a friend," I reply. "Not a personal friend of mine, but she knows my uncle. He asked a few people to keep an eye on me, that's all."

"You're all about friends and family, aren't you?" Abe asks with a shake of his head.

"It's not so strange when you break it down. My step-sister Jade is a cop. She told me one night when I called her that a lot of the offi-cers actually like the brothers in the MC."

"Like you? Christ, man, what do they do, sneak in here at night and rub you down?" Abe asks in disbelief.

"Nah, man, not 'like us' that way. I mean, some may, but I was talking more about what we do. My MC has charters all over the place. And in the areas we operate, we help keep the peace. Anytime someone does something on our turf that, say, infringes on our inter-ests, we handle it. Usually without involving the judicial system.

"No cop will admit to liking vigilantes, but they operate within a strict set of rules that can sometimes tie their hands. We don't have that problem. I told you earlier what landed me in here. All the offi- cers working here know what I did, and if you asked them when they're off the clock, every one of them would tell you if it had been them, they would have done the same damned thing."

"So, as far as the criminals in here go, they've got you pegged as one of the 'good ones,' is that it?" Abe observes.

"Yeah, exactly. Like you said, man, the Savage Kings are all about family and friends."

Abe lays down on his bed, staring at the ceiling in thoughtful silence. After a few minutes of consideration, he looks back over to me. "You mentioned prospecting if someone wants to join the Savage Kings. Tell me more about it."

I shift around to get comfortable on my bed, trying to decide where to start. "It's a different process for each candidate, really," I begin. "I suppose the best way to explain it would just be to tell you about what I went through. You know, give you an idea of what sort of things we get asked to do, and kind of get a feel for my brothers. I wasn't always the badass you see today." I chuckle. I pause a moment, gathering my thoughts, then I ask him, "You sure you want to hear all of this?"

"You got something else pressing to do?" Abe jokes.

"Ha! Good point. Well, first of all, you have to be eighteen. My eighteenth birthday came just after Christmas..."

CHAPTER TWO

2008

I look up when I hear the gravel crunching in the driveway. Seeing my Uncle Deacon's oversized Ford Bronco pulling into the yard, I straighten and hang the towel I was using to polish my bike over the handlebars. Climbing the porch steps as he gets out of the truck, I peer into the front window to see if my stepmom has set breakfast out on the table yet.

"Morning, Uncle Deacon!" I yell across the yard, loud enough that my parents can also hear me through the window. "Looks like you're just in time for breakfast if you're hungry."

"Hey, boy." Deacon stomps up the steps to join me. "Feels like it's gonna be a warm day, considering it's already January. You thinkin' about trying to get that junker over there running?" he asks, nodding towards my motorcycle.

"I'm not just thinking about it. I spent the last week tearing down that engine and rebuilding it. You want to hear it?" I ask, eager to impress my uncle, the president and one of the founding members of the Savage Kings MC.

"You really got that thing running?" Deacon asks me with a raised eyebrow. "Isn't that the old Electra Glide Eddie wrecked years ago? Last time I saw it, Turtle had it set off to the side at the salvage yard. He never had the heart to crush the damned thing."

"That's the one," I confirm. "I asked Eddie if I could work on it, and he told me I could have it if I could actually repair it."

"Well yeah, the engine was seized up and the stabilizer bar on the front fork was busted, just for starters. It would have cost more than the damned thing was worth to restore it."

"Yeah, I didn't really have the money for a 'restoration.' Now, don't be mad at Turtle, but he let me do some work around the scrapyard in exchange for some parts. I ended up putting an old panhead engine in it. As far as the forks, I welded two new stabilizer bars in, over and under the broken one, to compensate."

Deacon had walked over to the bike while I was talking, and I trail off as he circles it, casting a critical eye over the work I've done. "Well," he finally says with a sigh. "She ain't gonna win any award shows, but I can tell you I've seen a hell of a lot worse. I'm proud of you, Chase. Took a lot of initiative, and a lot of good work to get this done."

The screen door on the front porch closes with a bang, and we both glance over as my father comes down the stairs to join us. "I'm still not sure how I feel about you taking off on that thing," my dad says with a sigh, casting a skeptical eye at my bike. "But you're eighteen now, and I'm not going to stop you. You two come on in the house and get some breakfast. What brings you out here so early this morning?" my father asks his brother.

"Brought a present for the birthday boy," Deacon replies. "Let me go get it out of the truck."

My father and I go into the house and sit down at the table where my stepmom is already drinking her coffee. A moment later, Deacon comes in with a large flat box under his arm, setting it down on the table by me as he takes a seat.

"Morning, Carol," Deacon says with a nod in her direction.

She replies with a small smile as I stuff a piece of bacon into my mouth and rip the paper off the package. "Sorry I couldn't be here for your party, Chase," Deacon says as I break open the tape and lift the lid on the box. "The MC had a run planned, and besides, at your age, I figured you didn't want an old man lurking around your school friends."

"There wasn't any real party Saturday," my dad tells Deacon. "We had dinner together, and Chase went out with some of his friends, there was no big get together."

"That's a shame," Deacon grins. "We had a pig-pickin' out at the clubhouse for my fortieth last year, it was a big old time. You guys should come out next year, you know you're always welcome."

"And you know how I feel about the club," my dad sighs. "And so do you, Chase," he adds, as he watches me stand and hold up the present Deacon brought me.

It's a leather riding vest, brand new and unadorned on the front. Turning it around, I see that it does have one decoration on the back —a white patch that has been hand-stitched to the lower back, reading 'Prospect.' Before I can say a word, Deacon stands up with me.

"You remember asking me a while back when you could prospect with the MC? You had just failed your sophomore year of high school for skipping all those days, and not taking your responsibilities seriously. I told you then that if you couldn't man up and handle your business, you'd never have a place with us. Your daddy tells me you're a good student now, and that you've really turned things around. Fast Eddie said you'd asked after his old bike, and when we saw the work you were putting in, well, we took it to the table. The vote was unanimous. If you're still interested, I'm here as your sponsor to officially welcome you as a prospect with the Savage Kings."

"Deacon!" my dad snaps as he jumps to his feet. "You should have told me this was the 'gift' you were planning!"

"Why?" Deacon asks, obviously confused as he turns to face my father. He looks to my stepmom when he sees my dad's face going bright red. "Carol, what's the problem?"

"You know what the damn problem is, Deacon!" my dad yells. "Torin is already hell-bent on this prospecting business once he gets back from his service, but I'll be damned if you're going to bully my youngest into your insanity!"

I can feel my teeth grinding as my father continues to yell. I shake the vest once to straighten it out, then stretch to the full extent of my long, lean frame as I make a show of putting it on and zipping it. My father shuts up instantly, glaring at me.

"I'm not bullying anyone. Chase is a grown man now and can make his own decisions," Deacon says into the silence.

"There's no reason to be mad, Pops," I reassure my father. "You've known for a long time that I wanted to join the MC once I was old enough."

My father lets out another loud sigh and seems to deflate a bit as he sits back down at the table. "I know, Chase, but you have to remember, I've been around those guys a lot longer than you have. There's a reason I never let Deacon talk me into signing on with his gang. It's a dangerous lifestyle, and it's no place for a man who plans on having a family. I know it might seem like some glamorous exciting life, but..."

"I'm not looking at it as a lifestyle," I explain. "I'm looking at it as a career choice. Come on, Pops, you have to admit that Uncle Deacon and the club own or operate half the businesses in Emerald Isle. Let's be real, I'm not college-bound. You know I'm not higher education material. I've never liked school or had any academic ambitions."

"That's one of the reasons I'm so excited about you and your brother joining," Deacon adds. "We've spent years setting up legitimate businesses and making Emerald Isle a biker tourist attraction.

We've made good money, and with you two growing up around the club, and the area, you've both got good heads for how to help continue to build this MC."

"I don't like it," my father says in a flat voice. "But if you're intent on doing this, I can't stop you. I'm not going to throw you out or do anything crazy. I just want you to remember through this 'prospecting' business, that you can hang that cut up anytime and call it quits. Don't let them suck you into things that will land you in jail, or get you hurt, you understand?"

Deacon nods before he turns his attention back to me. "Your daddy's right, Chase. Prospects quit all the time if the lifestyle doesn't suit them. Usually happens during their training with old Eddie and Turtle, but I don't think you'll have much trouble with them. You planning on riding that bike of yours to school today?"

"Yeah, it's going to be warm, up in the sixties today. That's actually why Jade isn't here. She usually rides with me to school if I'm taking the truck, but since I got my bike running, she had to catch the bus."

"You going to bring your sister home this afternoon, or is she scared of that thing?" Deacon chuckles.

"She's going to get a ride home with a friend. She doesn't want anything to do with me or my bike," I sigh.

"In that case, once you're done, meet me out at the clubhouse this afternoon. I'll take you over to the scrapyard and drop you off with Turtle. He's not a member of the club, but he runs our towing business. You'll be working with him at first."

"Working?" I ask Deacon with a raised eyebrow.

"That's what I said," Deacon confirms. "Don't worry, you'll be paid, and not just in parts this time. Part of prospecting is getting an overview of all of our operations."

"All right," I agree, then wrap my uncle up in a fierce hug. "Thank you for this opportunity. I'm not going to let you down or embarrass you."

Deacon slaps me on the back, then pushes me back to look me up

25

and down with a smile on his face. "I know you won't, boy. Once we put some meat on you and you fill out that cut, you're going to make a damn fine member of the MC. Now get out of here. Part of your prospecting is going to involve you finishing school, you hear me?"

"Yes, sir." I nod, then bend down to kiss Carol on top of her head, before turning to my dad.

"Come on home tonight, once you're done out at Turtle's," he says gruffly. "We'll sit down over dinner, and you can tell me all about it. I worry about you, Chase, but I do support you. Be careful on that bike, all right?"

I give him a hug, then Deacon and I head outside. I zip up my leather riding jacket over my new cut, then retrieve my helmet. "I'll be out there to meet you by four this afternoon," I confirm with Deacon as I straddle my bike.

"Good! And hey, Chase, do me a favor and keep your eyes open out at your school." Deacon has to yell as I crank up my bike, its thunderous cough sending birds screeching into the sky all across the yard.

"What?" I yell back at him.

"Wearing that cut, I want you to pay close attention at school, see if anybody acts weird or avoids you, understand?"

"Not really, but I'll do it," I yell back to him. I don't know why anyone would give a prospect cut a second glance in our neighborhood. Everyone around here knows the Savage Kings MC, and for the most part, they're well-respected in the community. Still, my uncle...no, my president asked me to do it, so I'll keep my head on a swivel and see if anyone gives me the stink-eye.

With a final wave, I drop my bike into gear and ease down the gravel driveway. It's chilly this early in the morning, but not nearly enough to cool my enthusiasm or excitement for the day.

CHAPTER THREE

One of the reasons I was able to turn my grades around is that my high school lets students choose 'career-training' electives. Most people choose typing, or some sort of computer-related curriculum. Fortunately for me, they also have a fully-equipped garage where they taught what we all just call 'shop.'

I still have to deal with a literature and math class in the afternoon, but for a few hours every morning, I actually get to enjoy being at school. It's almost eight o'clock when I pull my motorcycle around the back of the shop, bringing it right up to the curb at the edge of the small parking lot. I kill the engine and then wave a greeting to my teacher, Mr. Aikens, who's sitting on the back step, tapping his pipe.

I hang my helmet on the handlebars, then walk over and take a seat beside him. "Good morning, Mr. Aikens," I greet him, as I pulled out a pack of cigarettes.

Mr. Aikens flicks a match and holds it down into the bowl of his pipe, puffing gently until it catches. When I lean towards him, he lifts up the match and lights my cigarette. "We're not supposed to be smoking out here, Fury," he says with a chuckle. "I'll let you slide this time, though, what do you say?"

"You've been letting me slide for two years, sir. I figure one more day won't hurt, will it?"

"Won't hurt at all," he agrees. We sit on the stoop and smoke in silence for a minute, the chill in the morning air causing our smoke and our breath to blend into a sparkling haze.

"Cold morning to ride that motorcycle," Mr. Aikens observes.

"It's going to warm up later. I just finished rebuilding it over the holiday and couldn't wait to bring it out to show it off."

"Looks like you did good work putting that junker back together."

I grin over at my teacher, pleased with the rare compliment. Mr. Aikens is a retired diesel mechanic and all-around handyman. He's normally so laid-back he seems about to fall over, but he's extremely critical of what he calls 'half-ass rigging' on our projects.

"Thank you, sir. I couldn't have done it without some of the things you taught in class."

"Hmph." Mr. Aikens snorts around his pipe-stem. "I'm glad to hear it. Got a special project for the automotive technology group this semester, and you'll need to be at your best for this one."

Before he can explain any further, he takes his pipe and begins tapping the ash out of the bowl on the step. More students were pulling into the parking lot, and as they start getting out of their cars, Mr. Aikens moves up the stairs to head inside. "Come on in when you're ready, Fury, and we'll get started with the introductions."

"Introductions?" I ask, but the door is already banging closed behind my teacher.

All of the guys in my class had been here for the entirety of this school year, if not longer. If we were getting a new student, I hoped they had a solid pair of stones on them. A lot of these old country boys I had class with liked to play rough with each other and had only started leaving me alone after I thumped a couple of them.

I grind out my cigarette on the step and go into the garage to size up the new guy for myself.

Inside, I hang up my leather jacket but leave on the new cut

Deacon had given me on over my t-shirt. My classmates were already gathering around a car that had been pulled into the garage, and I drew closer so I could hear Mr. Aikens over their excited chatter.

"...will be joining our class this semester. As you can see, she's been gracious enough to bring us a project. Miss Sheridan, why don't you tell everyone about your car?"

I had been eyeing the old rusty hulk parked in our garage, just like the rest of the class, when my attention was suddenly distracted by an angel descending upon us. As she stepped forward, her long blonde hair floated around her shoulders. Her lips were slightly parted in an excited smile as she faced the class, and her blue eyes sparkled in the overhead lights as she looked around, casting her spell over all of us.

"Hello everyone, I'm Sasha," she says, her melodic voice instantly bringing a hush over the normally rowdy group of guys surrounding her. "And this is my Mustang! I've been working on her with my dad in our spare time for the last few months. When I moved out here and saw that this school offered an automotive technology class, I got in touch with Mr. Aikens to see if the class might want to help me with the body work. I'm hoping that it will be a good learning experience for all of us, and I'm *really* hoping that you guys will help me turn her into something special!"

"Oh man. I can't wait to strip her down. Yo, Chase, how long do you think it will take?" Robbie asks me.

"You think you're ever going to get a single stitch off of her?" I growl, heat rising in my face at the thought of Robbie *fucking* Davies even laying a finger on this goddess.

"Nah, Mr. Aikens probably won't let us do it personally." Robbie sighs. My flare of anger sputters in confusion before being completely snuffed out by a chuckle.

"Oh man, I see what you're saying, Robbie. Go ask her and Mr. Aikens. I'm sure they'll let you help out with it. I'm going to see if I can too." I slap him on the shoulder to get him moving and push my way past a couple of the other guys to approach her.

I smile at her as she turns from our teacher and locks eyes with me. "We wanted to say thank you, and introduce ourselves." I hold out my hand to grasp hers. She's got some calluses on her palm and a streak of grease on her arm that disappears under the sleeve of her tight sweater. For a moment, I wonder how far up that smear runs, and what it would feel like to rub her clean. I force my gaze back up to her eyes, determined not to think about what else is going on under her sweater. "I'm Chase, Chase Fury. This is my friend, Robbie," I tell her, jabbing a finger behind me.

"This car is amazing," Robbie says, not even turning to face Sasha. "Please let me help with the body work!"

"Of course!" she says, with a smile that chases every bit of the chill from my morning ride right out of my body. "What about you, Chase Fury? Do you want to sign on for this project too, or are you going to stick to the normal coursework?"

When she speaks to me, my gaze fixates on her lips, and what I'm sure must be a voice gifted from heaven above. "I want to stick with you...your project," I stammer, realizing I'm staring again. "Miss Sheridan, was it? I didn't hear your last name clearly during the introduction."

"Sasha, Sasha Sheridan. Please don't call me Miss. It's just too strange coming from a guy in a leather vest," she replies with a laugh.

"Yeah, Chase, what gives with this thing?" Robbie asks from behind me. "What does this patch mean—'Prospect'? Oh, wait... Prospect...oh shit, Chase, sorry man, I didn't realize!"

"It's all right, Robbie, calm down," I reassure him. Poor kid thinks I'm going to slap him upside the head for insulting my cut. Which I would do, in a normal situation, if someone actually meant it. Out here at school, though, most of my classmates don't know the significance of it, and just think it looks strange.

"It's a bold fashion strategy, Cotton," Sasha drawls in an odd voice. "We'll have to stay tuned and see if it pays off!"

Robbie laughs from behind me, and as I turn to him with a scowl, he says to Sasha, "I got that reference, good one!"

Sasha smiles at my confusion. "You ever seen the movie *Dodgeball?*"

"No," I reply in a gruff voice, annoyed that Robbie got the joke.

"What, never? You too cool for movies, Mr. Fury?" Sasha teases.

"Of course not," I protest. "Just a couple of weeks ago, I saw..." I trail off, feeling my face flush slightly.

"Saw what?" Sasha prompts.

"Uhm...*Harry Potter,*" I mumble.

Sasha steps back and looks me up and down, taking in my dirty jeans, scuffed up combat boots, and the Motorhead t-shirt I'm wearing under my brand-new cut. Cracking a grin, she says, "I love *Harry Potter!* Those stories really appeal to all types of people, don't they?"

Before I can answer, Mr. Aikens interrupts us. "You guys can talk more while you're working. Sasha, you've had a chance to talk to your classmates. You can pick two at a time to work with you, we'll rotate around so everyone gets to be a part of the project. Who do you want to start with?"

Every guy in the class gets quiet as Mr. Aikens makes this announcement, practically holding their breath to see who will be the first to get to worship this angel. I don't realize I'm doing the same, right up until Sasha nods at me.

"Let me get this one, and his friend, Robbie, over there, to help me get started."

"All right, Chase, you and Robbie use your time today to go over the car with Sasha and let her give you an overview of the work it's going to need. Then we'll have a lesson for the entire class about the tools you'll use, and..."

Mr. Aikens's words are drowned out by my pulse thundering in my ears as Sasha walks past me to her car. She's tall, just a few inches shorter than I am, and when I breathe in her sweet apple scent, I feel an electric surge throughout my body, a jolt so powerful I visibly twitch. With a shudder, I get control of myself and turn to follow her.

Her Mustang is parked over our pit, which Robbie has already climbed down into. "I'm going to check out the undercarriage and try to see what kind of work we'll need to do!" he calls up to us.

"Where do you want to start?" Sasha asks me as she climbs into the driver's seat, then pops the hood.

"Well, let's take a look at...good Lord," I gasp, lifting the hood.

Sasha grabs a spotlight from the toolbox, then comes around to stand beside me. "Yeah," she agrees solemnly. "It's beautiful, isn't it?"

"Chase, you gotta check this thing out!" Robbie calls from under our feet. "The axles are new, and so is the transmission. This thing is beautiful!"

"You should take a look at the engine!" I yell down to him. "That is not a stock motor," I tell Sasha, looking over to see her smiling at my reaction.

"It most certainly is not," she agrees. "That's a 475-horsepower coyote crate engine my dad bought me for my seventeenth birthday. I installed the supercharger, right there." She shines the spotlight across the engine. "I mean, I had to get some help at my dad's garage to do the whole installation with the new transmission, but it's coming along well. My dad had the idea of bringing it down to the school to complete the body work. He thought it would be a good way to break the ice since I'm new around here."

"Who are you?" I ask, even more amazed by this angelic woman.

"I told you, goofball, my name is Sasha Sheridan," she says with a roll of her eyes.

"I got that part," I chuckle. "I mean, tell me about yourself. Look around, there are no women in the automotive technology program here. You should be, ah, I don't know, like a fish out of water. But you, you're a straight-up killer, a shark among goldfish. This car is damn impressive!"

"What can I say? I love Mustangs," she tells me, blushing and turning her head. "My dad owns a bunch of Ford dealerships up the East Coast. He moved down here a couple of months ago to set up a new location, and the rest of my family followed him over the Christmas holiday. My dad and I both love cars. He's done a few restoration projects in the past. This one is for me. We used the garages at his dealerships to do a lot of the initial work and get this baby running, but it still needs a ton of body work. So, like I said, my dad thought it would be a good idea to bring it over here and use it as a conversation starter, help me meet people."

"I'm not sure if your daddy is going to like the kind of people this hot rod will attract," I observe.

"People like you?" Sasha teases.

"Oh, god no," I protest, watching her smile slip slightly at the rejection. "Your parents would love me to death," I add, immediately bringing back her blush. "I am, after all, a perfect gentleman."

"Yeah, right." She snorts out a laugh, then immediately covers her mouth in embarrassment.

"Shine your light over here a moment, please," I tell Sasha as I notice something down in the engine compartment. "Has she been vibrating some when you open her up, or cruising on the highway?"

"Yeah, actually. When I get it up to speed, it's like trying to drive a bull," she says, leaning in with the spotlight.

"See that slight cracking right there?" I tell her, pointing down the side of the engine compartment.

Sasha steps closer to me, trying to see, then passes me the spotlight and leans over to get a better look. When she does, her sweater presses against my bare arm, and I realize her breast is resting on the back of my hand. I jerk my arm back as if it burned me.

"Shit, sorry," I blurt out.

"Oh, for fuck's sake," she replies with a laugh, the curse word falling from her mouth so naturally that I just stare at her in shock. She grabs my hand and pulls me back towards the car. "Stop acting like you've never seen a woman before and show me what's wrong with the freakin' car."

"I've never met anyone like you," I mumble, before shining the light back down into the engine compartment. "That crack right down there? The engine mount is broken. That's causing the vibration. Probably just an age issue. All this power needs more support than this old frame can provide."

"For now," Sasha adds with a grin.

"For now," I confirm. "I'll start writing it up for the class. We can pull the engine and figure out what it will need to repair the body, then with some grinding, welding, and painting, you'll be ready to take this monster down to the short track."

"How long do you think it will take, overall?" Sasha asks me.

"Eh, with this bunch of yahoos? Probably a few weeks. Mr. Aikens will want to use every piece as a test, watch and see."

"That's fine. I would really like to have it done before the end of February, if possible. That's when I turn eighteen, and having the Mustang finished has been my dream for a while. How about you?"

"You mean, how old am I? Or what car do I dream of? I just turned eighteen a week ago, right after Christmas. As to the second part, I use my dad's old truck sometimes, but whenever it's not freezing outside, I ride my bike," I tell her with pride.

"What, like a ten-speed? You ride that all over town?"

I just stare at her for a long moment before I realize she's not screwing with me, and that this is a serious question. "No, goofball," I finally reply with a laugh, throwing the charming insult back at her. "My bike, my motorcycle. Do I look like the Lance Armstrong type?"

She steps back and puts her hands on her hips, looking me up and down. "Not really, no. You look like you've got all your parts."

That makes me blush, because my first thought is that she's referring to Armstrong only having one ball. Was she checking out my package? Is it that noticeable in my jeans? Without thinking, I blurt out, "Do you want to see it?"

Her mouth falls open in shock before she breaks into a huge grin. "Do you really think this is the best place for you to show off all your parts?"

"No, I meant my motorcycle!" I protest, certain now that she was checking me out. I've had girls flirt with me before, but none have ever left me so flustered and off-balance. "Come on, it's just out back," I tell her, hoping the cool morning air will clear my head a bit.

She follows me outside and down the stairs to where my bike is parked against the curb. I swing a leg over the seat and stand it up, then ask her, "What do you think?"

Instead of gushing over it, or saying anything at all, she walks a full circle around me and then kneels down by my leg. "I think that it's unique, I'll give you that. This wasn't put together in any official Harley-Davidson factory, was it?"

I lean the bike back over before I dismount, then sigh in chagrin. "Is it that obvious? I couldn't afford even a used one working part-time around here, so I salvaged parts from all over to rebuild this thing. Tell me the truth, is it an embarrassment?"

"No, god no," Sasha says as she stands up. "Are you kidding? I mean, yeah, it won't win any awards for style, but mechanically, you did a great job. Did you do all this yourself, even painting the tanks and fenders?"

"Yeah, the club has a garage with all the equipment I needed, even an airbrush for the touch-up work."

"The club?" Sasha asks with a raised eyebrow.

"Yeah, the motorcycle club I'm prospecting with," I confirm, turning around to show her the 'Prospect' patch on the back of my vest. "The Savage Kings. They've got charters all up and down the East Coast, but the local group are the originals. My uncle is the president."

"Your uncle...is his name Bishop or...?" Sasha asked.

"Deacon," I reply with a laugh since her guess was also a church position. "Deacon Fury. He actually just invited me to prospect with them this morning. I've got to go out to meet with him later today."

"Deacon! That was it! My dad was telling us about him over dinner the other night!" Sasha says, catching me by surprise.

"How does your dad know my uncle?" I ask her in confusion.

"My dad was down here getting ready for the opening of his new dealership, when a group of guys on motorcycles roared onto the lot.

He said they made him nervous at first, but that a man named Deacon introduced himself as the president and wanted to welcome him to the neighborhood. My dad thought it was going to be an extortion racket or something, but he told us the bikers were actually cool and invited him to set up a booth at a charity event they have coming up, so he could show off some cars. They also told him about the towing company and salvage yard they run nearby," she explains. "My dad liked the guys so much, he signed contracts to let them handle any towing and repossessions he needs done out here."

I snort at that. "Well, if he needs those services around here, he probably didn't have much choice. The club has a bit of a monopoly in the area for that kind of work."

"At least they were nice about it!" Sasha laughs, picking up the helmet I left hanging on the handlebar. "So, when are you going to take me for a ride?" she asks, plopping the helmet on her head.

I walk around to her and gently lift the helmet back off of her. "I've never had anyone ride with me before," I admit. "I don't even have an extra helmet. Would you really want to risk riding with someone like me?"

"I don't know the risk," she says with a mischievous grin. "Because I don't know anyone like you. I tell you what, let me hold your phone and I'll give you my number. That is, if you want to hang out sometime and let me learn more about how 'risky' you are."

"I'd like that," I tell her. God, if the club could see me fawning over this woman like a damned fool, they'd revoke my offer to prospect. I hand her the flip phone I carry around, and she quickly punches in her name and number.

"When should I expect a call?" Sasha asks. "I'm new here, and with all the attention I've been getting..." She trails off as her phone begins to chime in her pocket.

She pulls the phone out of the butt pocket of the tight jeans she was wearing, her forehead crinkling as she stares at the unknown number on the screen. Then, looking up and noticing that I'm still holding my phone open in my hand, she smiles and answers the call with a flourish. "Hello there, this is Sasha speaking," she drawls, her voice echoing back from the speaker in my hand.

"Hi Sasha, this is Chase," I reply, stepping closer to her. We're so close our toes are almost touching, and our two phones begin to break up in static. "I was just calling to see if you would be interested in going for a ride with me tomorrow. I'll need time to get you a decent helmet, but assuming this weather holds, tomorrow should be a good day for it."

"Then it's a date," Sasha responds with a smile, ending the call and sliding her phone back into her pocket. "It will be good to get to know each other outside of class. I'm going to try to be all business in there while we're working on my baby. Come on, let's get back in there and get our plan written up for Mr. Aikens. You seem like you know what you're doing, Chase Fury, and together, I think we can make something beautiful."

"I hope so," I tell her as I linger a moment, letting her get ahead of me. I watch her walk up the stairs before I draw out a cigarette, needing a smoke to help calm my nerves. I've hung out with my Uncle Deacon at his clubhouse and seen the kinds of women the Savage Kings keep around. None of them have ever made me feel a fraction of what Sasha has in only these few moments. "We're not just going to make something beautiful," I vow to myself. "We're going to make something eternal."

CHAPTER FOUR

S asha and I can't help but flirt with each other throughout the morning. We're separated all too soon as first period ends, and it turns out we don't have any afternoon classes together. I don't see her as I walk across the campus to get to my bike, so with a tinge of regret, I pull out of the lot and try to clear my head as I ride to the Savage Kings' clubhouse. It will be my first time showing up as an official prospect, not just a hang-around, and I need to make sure I'm on top of my game.

When I rumble into the parking lot, I can't help but breathe a small sigh of relief. My Uncle Deacon's truck is here, along with a couple of other vehicles, but only one motorcycle. A lot of guys 'winterize' their bikes, pulling out the batteries and putting them on trickle chargers, or even leaving them up on jacks so the tires don't get flat spots. I'm still self-conscious about my franken-bike, and the thought of putting it in line with the kinds of rides my brothers own has me sweating bullets.

I pull in beside the new Dyna Glide low rider sitting near the door, taking a moment to eye it enviously. I haven't seen the bike before, but I haven't been around the clubhouse enough to even meet all the members, much less get familiar with all their bikes. Hanging up my helmet and sunglasses, I walk to the front door inlaid with the Savage Kings logo, then with a deep steadying breath, step inside.

The front room is huge, spotted with tables for playing cards and drinking. Two pool tables dominate the center, while the bar itself runs along the back of the room. A couple of men I don't know are playing darts, while my Uncle Deacon is sitting beside one of the club members at a table, looking at something on a laptop. I think the woman behind the bar is Lori, one of the girls who hangs around the club frequently. She's trimmed her blonde hair into a short pixie cut since the last time I saw her, so it takes me a moment to recognize her. When she spots me standing in the doorway, she puts down the case of beer she was carrying and runs towards me with a squeal.

"Chase, oh my god, look at you in your cut! Deacon said you were starting today as a prospect! I'm so excited!" she gushes as she wraps me in a hug.

"Thanks, Lori," I tell her, while scowling over her shoulder. This isn't how I wanted to make my first entrance to the clubhouse. I hug her back, and when she pulls away, I smile at her. She's been hanging around the club for over a year, and when Deacon first started letting me come over and shoot pool, Lori was very...welcoming.

"I know you've probably got stuff to do on your first day, but when you get done, come back later and we'll celebrate together," Lori says. Then, leaning over to press her tits into my arm, she whispers, "We're going to make your first day unforgettable, baby."

She lifts her head to try and kiss me, but fortunately, Deacon intervenes at that exact moment. "Hey Lori, let me get one for the road before Chase and I head out, will you?"

"Sure thing, Deacon!" she replies, before turning back to me and mouthing, "Later, baby."

Once she goes back behind the bar, I walk over and take a seat with Deacon and the other club member, who I recognize as Reese, a former soldier who just earned his cut recently.

"You remember Reese, don't you, Chase?" Deacon says by way of introduction.

"Yeah, we've played pool a couple of times while he was prospecting," I confirm.

Reese doesn't look up from whatever he's doing on his laptop, but does give a nod of his head, which I assume is a greeting from the normally quiet man.

"Reese only got his top rocker recently, so he's going to be working with you during your prospecting period. You'll meet up with him at the scrapyard later this evening, after Turtle brings you back from a run. Turtle and Eddie have been out doing some repossessions today, but they've got one they saved so you could ride along."

"That sounds good to me. What will I be doing day-to-day while I'm prospecting, exactly? I mean, you know I've still got school most of the day. You want me to ride out here every afternoon?"

"Nah, that won't be necessary," Deacon tells me. "Most days after school, you can head over to the scrapyard to meet up with Turtle and Eddie. They're going to show you the ins and outs of some of our businesses. Reese will meet you out there most days for other kinds of training. I wanted you to come out here today so I could show you around the members-only areas of the clubhouse." Turning to Reese, Deacon asks, "You got him all set up in our system?"

Reese nods to Deacon, then turns to speak to me. "You should be getting a text," he says cryptically.

My phone vibrates instantly, so I flip it open to see a short text with a four-digit code. "What's this for?" I ask Reese.

"That's the passcode to the basement areas, the part of the club that is off-limits to the general public," Deacon replies. Reese is already packing up his laptop, and as he stands from the table, Deacon continues, "He's probably going back to his room, so come on, and I'll show you the downstairs area. You'll have a room down there, if you ever need a place to crash."

"You stay down there?" I ask Reese before he can turn to walk away. He nods to me, then heads over to a door at the side of the room, pointing at a keypad on the wall before punching in a code and disappearing.

"Is he quiet around everyone, or did I do something?" I ask Deacon.

Deacon sighs, then finishes off the beer Lori had brought him earlier. "He's always like that around new people. He's a homebody and spends most of his time downstairs with his toys. He's never what I'd call chatty, but he'll open up a bit once he gets used to you."

"His toys?" I ask, as we both get up from the table and go over to the heavy sealed door guarded by the keypad.

"Yeah, he's got one hell of a computer rig set up down there. That boy can find out anything from the workshop he's got in his room. It's kinda frightening, really, when I think about it. I suppose that's part of what brought him to us, when you get down to it. He's curious about everything, and he's got the skills to find answers. Answers to questions most people know better than to ask, and answers that can get you in trouble. I guess we're all like that, in one way or another," Deacon continues, after punching in the code and leading me down a well-lit set of stairs. "None of us Kings fit into polite society, each in our own peculiar way."

The stairway ends in a long hallway, with multiple doors on each side. Leading me all the way down the left-hand hall, he opens up a heavy wooden door inlaid with the Savage Kings' skull logo. "This is the chapel, where we hold our club meetings," Deacon says, waving an arm for me to go in and take a look around.

It's a long, narrow room dominated by a huge intricately carved oak table. Over a dozen chairs sit around haphazardly, as though the men who were in them got up and left in a hurry. The walls are hung with all sorts of plaques and banners depicting races and rallies the club has attended or hosted.

After I take a moment to absorb the sight, Deacon touches my arm and leads me back down the hall. "As a prospect, you'll only enter the chapel when you're invited, understand? All of these other rooms will be off-limits without an invitation as well, except for this one."

Deacon stops at a door positioned almost directly across from the stairwell. "We keep two bedrooms set up for prospects. This one will be yours, whenever you need it. The sheets are clean and there's a bathroom attached, so don't hesitate to ever come here and crash. You're not a full brother yet, but you are family, you understand?"

"Thank you," I say in a hoarse voice, wrapping my uncle up in a hug. "I know what a big deal it is for you to nominate me personally, being the president and all. I'm not going to let you down."

"Aw hell, boy, I watched you grow up. I know the kind of man you've become," Deacon says, letting go of me and stepping back awkwardly. "Come on, let's head back upstairs. We'll ride over to the salvage yard and I'll turn you over to Eddie and Turtle."

"All right," I agree. "Turtle's not a member of the club, is he?" I ask, once we're back upstairs.

"He's not," Deacon confirms. "But that's only because he can't ride a motorcycle. He's a good friend, and I want you to obey him like a brother. Well, for the most part anyway. Turtle's never abused his position with us, but he is kind of odd sometimes. Artillery shell went off close to him back in the war, and he's got a plate in his head now. If he asks you to take a kitten home and foster it, just let a brother know and we'll handle it for you. You don't have to become part of his farm."

"Ha! Sounds like there is a story behind that. What happened?"

"Oh, nothing serious," Deacon replies. "Turtle got a wild hair up his ass while Reese was prospecting and gave the boy a box he swore were kittens. Wanted the boy to keep them for him, because Eddie wouldn't let him keep them at the scrapyard. Prospects normally can't say no to a request from a member or a friend of the club, so he just took the box without peeking in and loaded it up in the backseat of his car. He was on his way back to the bar when Eddie called us all worked up in a panic. Turned out the box was actually full of baby skunks, and Eddie had told Turtle to go set them loose back in the woods. We couldn't get hold of Reese on the phone, so we went out looking for him. Found him out on Highway Nine, puking over a guardrail. One of the little devils had gotten excited and let loose a spray while he was driving. Reese never did get that smell out of his car." Deacon chuckled.

"Damn, I'll keep that in mind then," I laugh. "Don't take any animals from Turtle. I'll follow you over there, okay?"

It doesn't take long for us to ride over to the scrapyard. Deacon parks his truck in the gravel lot and I take a moment to back my bike into a space beside him. There are two trucks in front of a huge four-bay garage, while the rest of the front lot is filled with vehicles that have been towed or repossessed, awaiting their owners. The scrapyard begins behind the garage and stretches off a couple of acres into the distance. After I get off my bike and stow my helmet, I see Turtle inside the first bay, bending down to mess with something on the ground. A moment later, a small furry object shoots out of the garage. A tiny white and brown bulldog puppy runs up to me, its entire rear-end shaking in joy.

I can't stop the grin that spreads across my face as I bend down and pick him up, letting him lick my chin. Turtle comes out to meet us, leaning heavily on the cane in his right hand. "Hey boys!" he calls to us. "I see my little buddy has taken a liking to you, that's a good sign! Always good to get a little love from someone before you set off on a repo job. You ain't gonna get any while we work."

"Turtle's got one more repo to do today," Deacon says. "He'll show you the ins and outs of this part of the business over the next couple of weeks."

"You want me to come out here after school every afternoon?" I ask.

"Nah, not every day. Eddie or Reese will text you and let you know when to show up out here," Deacon clarifies. "Let me hold that puppy so you two can hit the road. What's his name?" he asks Turtle as he takes the dog from me.

"Ain't got no name yet," Turtle replies, spitting a line of tobacco juice into the parking lot. "He ain't done nothing yet except wag and lick, and I already got two dogs named that. He'll let me know his name eventually."

"Right." Deacon snorts. "Well, I'm going to go find Eddie. You two have fun out there. Reese is going to be here when you get back, Chase. You guys can figure out your schedule this week later on."

Still wrestling with the squirmy puppy, Deacon disappears into the garage. Turtle slaps me on the arm, then points to the truck nearest to us. "Go on around and get in. I'll crank her up and take us into town. We're picking up a Lincoln Navigator. Info I got says that it's out at the courthouse, owner has a divorce hearing today. We'll round it up while he's inside and be gone before anyone's the wiser."

I'm able to climb up into the truck easily, but Turtle takes a minute to get himself into the cab. While he's struggling to get his bum leg into position, the denim jacket he's wearing flaps open and I see the handle of a pistol sticking out from under his left arm.

"You expecting any trouble?" I ask him once he's settled, nodding to the gun.

"Always expecting it," he agrees. "Don't matter if you're a boy scout or a biker, 'be prepared' is a good motto to live by. We should be in town in fifteen minutes or so. You got any questions about this before we get there?"

"Not yet," I reply. "I've used a tow rope to pull cars out of ditches before, but I'll need you to show me how we get a truck up on the hook without damaging it, how the controls work, just simple stuff."

"Hell boy, it's easy. If I can do it, I know you'll pick it right up," Turtle says, picking up a Styrofoam cup from the console holder to spit out more tobacco juice.

"I guess I do have one question," I blurt out after a moment. "What's your name? All these years I've known you, and I've only ever heard you called Turtle-Head, or Turtle."

Glancing over at me and grinning, he says, "My Christian name is Eugene, or just Gene. No one's called me that since my momma died though, and even she thought Turtle-Head was a better name for me."

"How did you get that name? Deacon said you had a plate in your head or something."

"Yup. I was a sniper in Vietnam. Don't know if you've heard much about it, but the short of it is that we had orders to overrun a base out in the jungle. Weren't any good open areas, so I ended up having to shoot from tree cover. Trees are bad business for sniping."

I thought this over for a moment while Turtle spit again, then asked, "How so? I mean, you were a sniper. Seems like you would need the cover."

"Naw, hell no, boy," Turtle scoffs. "After my first shot, them boys knew which general direction I was shooting from, and they started lobbing mortars into the area. If you're out in the open, hiding in a field or some such, you only got to worry about a mortar landing right on you. If you're in the trees, every damn mortar that lands blows splinters and limbs every which-a-way. I didn't technically get hit by artillery fire, I got injured when a big ass tree blew up and fell on me. Knocked a hole in my damn skull and my leg. Heh, took a crew of engineers to get me out from under that thing."

"Man, it's a miracle you survived all that. Is that why you can't ride a motorcycle, your leg that bad?"

"Yeah, but honestly, I never had much interest in them anyhow. Or at least, since I'll never be able to ride, that's what I tell myself."

We drive in silence for a short time, before my curiosity gets the better of me again and I continue questioning him. "So, when did the whole 'Turtle' thing start, while you were recovering after getting a plate put in your skull?"

"Well, that was part of it. It started when I was in therapy. You might have noticed, I'm a bit slow now. I don't get around as well as I did before that tree went through my leg. When you're slow, stubborn, and got more metal than bone in your head, well...the name Turtle suits me just fine. We're almost to the courthouse, help me look for a gold Lincoln Navigator."

We cruise slowly through the crowded courthouse parking lot until we spot what looks like our target close to the front, in a handicapped parking space. "Well, that's inconvenient," Turtle mumbles as he pulls the tow truck around, then backs it towards the Lincoln. The back-up alarm beepers get the attention of everyone outside, causing me to feel an unusual nervous tremor all throughout my body.

"Hop on out, boy. We're going to confirm this is the right one, then hook her up," Turtle orders.

"How do we confirm it's the right one?" I ask as I climb down from the truck.

"Because the lienholder gave us a copy of the key from the dealer," Turtle explains as he goes to the driver's side door of the Navigator and unlocks it. "Then we check the VIN number in here to make sure it matches our paperwork, which you can see here it does, and we're on our way!"

"Don't we have to inform the owner that we're taking it?" I ask, as Turtle leads us back to the winch and begins unspooling the tow cable.

"We already did, two weeks ago. He's been hiding it ever since, pretty much dared us to come get it. That boy Reese is good at finding stuff though, so here we are," Turtle says, as he brings the hook over to the car, taking a moment to show me how to attach it underneath the frame to avoid causing any damage. "All right, now. You go drop her into neutral while I jack her up and pull her a bit closer, then we'll head on out of here. Easiest thing in the world, see?"

I nod in agreement then jump into the truck, following his instructions. I feel a twinge of guilt as I look at the handicapped placard hanging from the rearview mirror, but I quickly remind myself of what Turtle said. This guy has been on notice and had a chance to deal with this situation. Repossession is always a last resort.

Once the rear of the vehicle is in the air and it's been pulled partially out of the parking space, Turtle waves for me to come join him. I hop out of the Lincoln and close the door, then turn and almost run headlong into a man in a gray suit.

"What the fuck do you think you're doing?" he roars at me, spittle flying across my face.

I recoil, surprised and disgusted, then look over the man as I wipe a hand across my face. He's as tall as I am, well over six feet, and looks to be in his late thirties or early forties. His thick chest and shoulders are straining against the fabric of his suit as he breathes, and his face is red with rage. Despite his demeanor, the thing that really sticks to me about him is that he appears so...healthy.

"You don't look handicapped," I accuse him.

"What? You son-of-a-bitch! Put my truck down right now!" he screams.

"No," I tell him in a calm voice, trying not to escalate the situation. "We have a repossession order, and..."

Before I can get any further, the man surprises me again, throwing a short punch that hits me right in my eye. He follows up by bull-rushing me and knocking me to the ground, his greater weight easily knocking me off-balance. I scuttle backwards on the pavement, trying to get my feet under me to fight back, when the man suddenly grabs for the back of his head, standing up straight and turning as though he was hit from behind.

Sure enough, as he turns away from me I can see Turtle standing there, holding his cane, which he just used to bonk this guy on top of the head. Turtle is at least a head shorter than the truck's owner, and as old and out of shape as he looks, I know I'm about to see a massacre. I scramble to my feet just as the man yells again, and takes a wild swing, trying to knock Turtle's head off.

My jaw drops open when Turtle simply leans back slightly, the angry truck owner's fist narrowly missing his nose. Shifting his position slightly, Turtle brings his cane up between the man's legs, smashing his balls with so much force the man immediately drops to his knees, his breath wheezing out of him in a long squeal of pain. Turtle takes one limping step backward, then brings the cane around once more in a golf swing, sending the big man sprawling with a crushing blow to his jaw.

I'm still staring in awe when two of the police officers who man the courthouse entryway come running over to us, their tasers already drawn. Turtle is leaning on his cane again, looking for all the world like an old, overweight invalid.

"Everyone, stay where you are," the first officer orders all of us, as the second bends down to assess the man lying on the ground. "We saw part of what happened here, are you all right sir?" he asks Turtle.

"Yeah, I reckon I'm fine," Turtle drawls. "Got a repossession order for this SUV, and while my assistant was finishing up, this asshole came over and punched him."

The asshole in question was being propped up into a sitting position by the other officer. As soon as he hears Turtle speaking, his cheeks blossom into a red rage once again. "You saw that man beat me with a cane! Put him in handcuffs, arrest him, do something!"

"Sir, calm down," the second officer orders. "We saw him strike you in the back of the head with the cane before you tried to punch him. Were you defending yourself?"

"You're damn right I was," he roars.

"Now, boy," Turtle starts. "You, me, and Jesus all know that's a lie. You had already attacked my trainee over there, who's just a young'un, only sixteen years old. I had to defend the boy from a fight you started. If anyone should be under arrest, I reckon it's you."

"Is that true?" the first officer asks me.

I wasn't sure if Turtle actually knew how old I was, but I could see that part didn't really matter. "Yeah, we were just getting ready to leave with the truck, when this fellow blindsided me and knocked me upside the head." I touched the sensitive area just under my left eye, where I could already feel the bruised knot forming. "I'm going to have a hell of a black eye, feels like."

"So, you assaulted a minor who was working on repossessing your vehicle, and had to be subdued," the first officer summarizes. "Seems like we've got a pretty clear picture of what happened. I'm going to need to get your names and contact information, then we can let you two get on with your business. Go ahead and restrain him," he orders the other officer, nodding to the man still sitting on the ground.

"What? A minor, no, I..." the man begins to argue before the second officer interrupts him.

"You're under arrest. You have the right to remain silent..." he says as he pulls out his handcuffs.

Turtle was already scribbling down his contact information on a piece of paper as I approached him and the officer.

"I appreciate all your help here, sir, I truly do," Turtle says as he hands the paper over. "I'd appreciate it though, if you'd put the word in that we don't really want to press any charges. This sort of thing is just par for the course in our line of work, you understand. Wouldn't do to be missing a bunch of days dealing with legal proceedings and what-not."

"We'll hold onto him and let him cool off for a while, then we'll decide once we see how he acts," the officer replies. Then, to my surprise, he winks at Turtle! "We probably will cut him loose in a bit, though. It would be hard to make an assault on a minor charge stick, wouldn't it?"

"I reckon that if anyone looked real close, they might find the two of us are both a bit older than we appear," Turtle agrees as he reached over and clasps my shoulder. "Go ahead and hop on in the truck, boy, and let's get on out of here. Thanks again, officer."

I keep my mouth shut until we're pulling out of the courthouse parking lot, then I glance over at Turtle. "You do know I'm eighteen, right?"

"Heh," he snickers. "'Course I know that. Couldn't prospect if you weren't, that's just how the club works. That fool that hit you didn't know that, though, and if he thinks he'll get in trouble for smacking a kid, he'll cause less trouble."

"You seem pretty spry for an old fat man with a cane," I observe.

Turtle lets out a real belly laugh at that, then turns to look at me.

"It's an easy mistake for most folks to make. They don't know I'm an old soldier, and they don't expect I might have more than a little fight left in me. People tend to underestimate you biker boys, too, you know. Always thinking you're just some dumb old racist boys. Gives folks a hell of a shock when they realize how sophisticated the club really is. It's like that everywhere you go, I suppose. People are so full of themselves, always thinking they're smarter or better than anyone else in the room. You can take advantage of that, when you need to."

"What do we do now, just take this thing back to the lot and secure it?" I ask, to change the subject.

"That's it," Turtle agrees. "Then I'm going to hand you off to that Reese fella. He's going to meet up with us and show you some more of our facilities."

The way he said "facilities" sounded ominous, but instead of asking for any further details, I just look out the window and rub at my sore cheek, wondering what I should tell that golden-haired angel tomorrow at school. I'm going to have to come up with something a lot more heroic than what really transpired, or she'll laugh me out of class. The rest of the ride passes in silence as I dream up ways to spin my black eye into something that might impress her.

CHAPTER FIVE

When we arrive back at the scrapyard, a motorcycle is parked out front in the space beside mine. After we unhook the Lincoln Navigator and get it parked, Turtle walks me up to the front office, where he plops down heavily in a battered old rolling chair.

"Reese will be out back probably, just head on over through the garage and out that door," he says, pointing out the way to me.

"Thanks for all the help today, Turtle," I reply, reaching out to shake the old man's hand. I head through the garage and out the back door, where I find Reese sitting in a battered old folding chair, smoking a cigarette.

When he sees me, he gives me a nod, then stands up and walks over to me. He walks completely around me one time, stopping in front of me and reaching out to squeeze my upper arm, then poke me in the abdomen.

"What are you doing?" I ask in annoyance.

"You do any weightlifting?" Reese asks in reply.

"Yeah, I got a weight bench in my garage at home. Well, it belongs to my older brother Torin, but I use it all the time."

"You've got pretty muscle," Reese says. "Good for impressing girls. We're going to do some work together. You're going to get functional muscle, the kind that impresses men."

"I'm not trying to impress men." I snort. When Reese doesn't respond to the joke, I try to prompt him. "So, what, you're going to be my coach, or trainer?" I try to clarify.

"I'm going to be your brother," Reese says. "I want you to be worthy of it."

With that, he peels his shirt off, hanging it on the folding chair where he was sitting. I suddenly see what he means about functional muscle. Reese is as cut as I am, but he's got to be at least fifty pounds heavier, and he's thicker than I am all through his upper body.

"Take off your cut and shirt. Put on these," he orders, giving me a pair of safety goggles.

Once I strip down and strap on the goggles, he puts a pair on his head and leads me further into the scrapyard, into a section where crushed cars have been neatly stacked. He stops beside the battered remains of what looks like a Ford truck, its frame twisted from some distant trauma. Reaching into the truck's cab, Reese pulls out two massive sledgehammers, throwing one over his shoulder while letting the head of the other crash down onto the dirt.

"That one's yours," he tells me, moving to the rear of the wrecked truck.

"Okay...what do you want me to do with it?" I ask in confusion.

"We strip everything we can use from these wrecks. Then we crush them. Like this!" Reese grunts, swinging the sledgehammer in a sideways arc into the truck's rear gate. The impact shatters the latch, and the gate booms open. Barely missing a beat, Reese swings again, overhanded, smashing the tailgate right off its hinges.

"That's not how the cars normally get crushed." I chuckle, awkwardly picking up the sledgehammer he left for me, then make sure my goggles are secure.

"I do it like this," Reese says. "Best exercise you can get. You start at the front." With that, he begins swinging at the rear fender, leaving huge dents in the sheet metal with each strike.

I move to the front of the mangled truck, then take an experimental swing, smashing a dent into the hood. With a grin, I wind up for another strike, this time knocking one side of the bumper into the dirt. "Ok, I get it. This is actually fun!" I yell back to Reese.

For the next fifteen minutes, I keep pace swing for swing, hammering away at the hood and front fenders until my hands begin to blister and burn. I finally let the head of the sledgehammer fall to the earth, then lean on it as I gasp for breath. The muscles in my arms and chest are vibrating like live wires, and the hammer feels like it's gained fifty pounds. "How long are you planning on keeping this up?" I yell to Reese.

"You stop when I stop," he grunts, still smashing the rear fenders.

"You do this for exercise every day?" I ask, trying to engage him in some sort of conversation while I recovered.

"No," he grunts in reply.

"What other things do you do to get 'manly muscles,' big guy? Wrestle bears? Coal mining, maybe?" I laugh.

Reese doesn't respond, but if the crushing force of his next few swings are any indication, he seems to be getting irritated. I pick my hammer back up and take another couple of swings, but my arms are so tired, the hammer just bounces back while barely leaving a mark. I move to the other side of the truck and keep at it for a few more minutes, until finally my trembling arms refuse to bring the hammer up past my shoulders.

"Seriously man, how long are you planning on keeping this up?" I ask Reese again as I walk back around the truck.

He's covered in sweat, but only pauses long enough to glare at me before taking another swing.

"Deacon told me you don't talk much, but you could at least answer my damn question!" I yell, my voice echoing through the scrapyard as Reese suddenly drops his hammer.

"I don't like repeating myself," he says, not looking at me. "I already told you, you're done when I'm done. I'm not done. Now, go get your hammer." With that, he stretches his arms over his head, twists to each side, then picks his sledge back up. Before he takes his next swing, he glances back at me and says, "I talk when I have something worth saying. You should try it. Or not. If you can't follow a simple order, leave."

"Leave? So that's what this bullshit is? Your way of seeing if I'll break if things get a little tough? Fuck you, man, I'll pound this goddamned wreck right down into the earth, and when I'm done, I'll shove this hammer up your ass!"

I've always had an explosive temper, and the strain of trying to be professional today while working with Turtle, coupled with the indignity of having this mute fucking freak belittle me, has pushed me past my breaking point. I snatch up my hammer, the muscles in my arms bulging with the pressure of my unrestrained fury. I walk past Reese and leap up onto the bed of the truck, cock the hammer over my shoulder and bring it down on the roof of the cab. Glass shatters outward several feet in every direction as the roof collapses inward, but I'm only getting started.

I'm so angry, my vision is blurry, while my ears fill with the roaring of my blood pounding through me. The hammer seems weightless as I rain blows down on the truck, the cab collapsing underneath my assault. I would have continued until I collapsed, but on my last swing, the head of the hammer misses the rear edge of the cab, the force of my blow landing high on the handle. Instead of the ringing of metal on metal, a crack like lightning striking a tree echoes around us, as the head of the hammer flies off into the scrapyard, leaving me holding only the jagged stump of the shaft.

I stand atop the wreck, gasping for breath, the fragment of the hammer's handle trembling in my grasp. I can feel my eyes bulging wildly as I turn to glare at Reese, waiting for him to hurl some insult at me. He doesn't say anything, however, and instead just looks at me with what I swear is the slightest hint of a smile.

"Broke my hammer," I finally sputter between gasps before

throwing the broken shaft out into the scrapyard. "You going to let me use yours?"

Without answering, Reese drops his hammer on the ground, then waves a hand for me to follow him. I jump down from the bed of the truck and fall in behind him, still sweating and panting for breath. My irritation, which had been slightly abated by my outburst, begins to rise again when I notice that Reese is still dry and not even breathing hard.

He leads me back to the garage, but instead of going into the open bay, he stops and unlocks a side door leading into an attached building I've never entered. Once we're inside, he flips on a bank of lights, the overhead fluorescent bulbs illuminating a large open room ringed by different exercise machines and free weights, with the center being dominated by a large thick gym mat.

"My job is to toughen up prospects, and make sure they can represent themselves well in any and all club activities," Reese says as I walk around the room.

"Represent themselves? You going to teach me some manners, show me which fork to eat with at the family table, shit like that?" I snort at him.

"I'm going to teach you to fight," Reese explains as he walks to the center of the mat. "First, you're going to hit me."

I size him up, trying to determine if he's fucking with me again. He just stands there with his arms hanging at his sides, looking as if he doesn't have a care in the world. I stalk over to him and say, "You remember you asked for this!" before I haul my right fist back and throw everything I have at him.

I feel his arm smack my forearm just before the world goes topsy-turvy, and I'm lying flat on my back on the mat. Reese had caught my punch and thrown me over his hip, before I could barely register he was moving!

I scramble to my feet, but Reese makes no sign of advancing on me. He just keeps staring at me blankly, until I charge back at him, this time coming in with my head low to wrap him up close. He raises his arms and leans forward as I slam into his belly, but instead of falling backward, he stands straight and stiff, a pure concrete wall against my hurricane.

I slam my fist into his side and kidney repeatedly until one of his arms snakes around my neck, then he falls to the floor, taking me with him. His grip around my neck tightens, choking me and causing an awful pressure to build up in my head. I thrash and pound his stomach, trying desperately to break free, but he might as well have been carved from granite. Just before I think I'm going to pass out, his arm lets loose and with a shove, he rolls me away from him.

By the time I get back to my feet, Reese has already gotten back up and walked a few feet away from me. "That was better than your first try," he comments. "But you don't want to try that move against someone who outweighs you as much as I do. If you don't knock them over right away, you end up vulnerable."

"I didn't know what else to try," I admit. "When I just tried to punch you, I got thrown down. I didn't know I was going to be learning some crazy biker judo."

"You're not," Reese replies. "It took me years of practice. I'm here to teach you to fight. First, I want you to understand this. Most of the people you will ever have a conflict with have no stomach for a fight, they'll do whatever they can to get away from it. Once I'm done with you, your presence alone will deter them. Most of the people you'll have a conflict with, who do have the stones to fight, don't know how to do it well. I'm not going to turn you into Bruce Lee in a biker jacket. I'm going to make sure that if you run into someone who has the balls to face you, you can beat them."

"That's not very encouraging. What am I supposed to do if I run into someone who wants to fight, can fight, and is actually better at it than I am?"

"Then you get your ass kicked until your brothers jump in," Reese says without a hint of humor. "The Savage Kings are a brotherhood. One of our bylaws is quite clear on this point. If a brother is in a fight with a non-club member, you have to join in."

"Then I wish I had some brothers here to help me with you." I laugh. "All I'm learning from you is how to lose."

"They wouldn't help you," Reese says seriously. "Fights between brothers are not bound by the same rules."

"Whatever, man," I scoff. "So, when does the learning to fight begin for real?"

"You're already learning. You learned not to rush someone much bigger than you, and you learned not to start your punch when you're so far away from me."

"What?" I try to clarify. "That's how you threw me at first, I was too far away?"

Reese walks over to me, only about a foot away. "A man who doesn't know how to fight will start the punch at a distance, because he doesn't want to get hit in return. Get that out of your head. If you get into a fight, you are going to get hit, and you're going to get hurt. There is no avoiding that. Once you commit to wanting to hit someone so badly that you don't care if you get hit back, you'll be in the right mindset."

"We're up in each other's faces, maybe cussing each other out, you know how it goes. Usually there's a shove or something that gets it all started," I comment, putting my palms to his chest and pushing lightly.

"You're not a bitch, you're a Savage King," Reese growls, slapping my hands away. "Don't ever wait for the other person to start the fight. If you know it's coming, you get close, as close as we are now, and you do *this*!" Reese brings his right fist up quicker than I could follow, just stopping to press his knuckles gently against my jaw. "Come over to the bag and I'll show you," he finishes.

Walking up to the heavy bag suspended from a chain in the ceiling, Reese gets close enough to hug it, then demonstrated a series of punches. He throws them in quick succession, sending the bag reeling away. He catches the bag in a one-armed hug as it returns, then motions for me to take over.

"What, I don't need to wrap my hands or something?" I quip.

Reese just stares at me with a frown, so with a shake of my head, I lay into the bag. I follow his lead, as he shows me a series of punches and then waits for me to repeat them. After a few repetitions, he backs away and waves for me to continue. When my knuckles begin to split open, he brings me two small towels that I wrap around my hands. I know better than to ask if we were finished, because he still hasn't said anything else.

After almost an hour of this, Reese finally pulls out a phone to check the time, then says, "Stop. You're off tomorrow to rest. Meet me at the clubhouse when you're done with school the next day, and we'll go from there."

He starts to walk away, but pauses when I ask, "Where are you going? Back to the clubhouse?"

He turns around and nods at me, then waits, assuming correctly that I would have another question.

"I'm wiped out, man. I don't know if I can ride my bike like this," I admit. I hold up my hands to show the tremors running through my arms and hands. "You worked the hell out of me today."

Reese gives me a sour look, but then says, "I can drive one of the tow trucks and take you to the clubhouse. Sleep there, and I'll bring you back for your bike in the morning."

"That's perfect. Thanks, man." I sigh. "Let me get my stuff." I follow him back outside to get my shirt and cut, then send a quick text to my dad that I'll be staying at the clubhouse tonight. After that, I climb into the passenger seat of the tow truck that Reese had idling out front, slumping wearily back into the cracked vinyl.

I don't bother trying to strike up any conversation, I'm just too tired. I crack my window to let in the cool night air as Reese drives us in silence through the dark back roads to the clubhouse, not even bothering to turn on the radio.

We've been on the road about ten minutes when Reese suddenly glances over at me and starts talking. "One day, this sweet little old lady walked into the clubhouse," he says. "She must have been in her eighties and was dressed in her Sunday best pantsuit. She looked around until she spotted the biggest, meanest-looking SOB in the place, and walked right up to him. She said, 'I want to join the Savage Kings.' Every one of us burst out laughing, but the brother she was talking to waved us to be quiet, because he wanted to have some fun with her. He asked her, 'Do you even own a bike?' She puffed up real proud and said, 'I certainly do. It's parked right out front.' The brother is surprised, so he asks her, 'Do you swear a lot?' 'Like a sailor with fucking syphilis,' she replies. 'Do you drink?' he asks her. 'Like a fish,' she tells him. Well, everyone is impressed now, so the brother asks her one more question. 'You ever been picked up by the fuzz?' She looks really thoughtful for a moment, then says, 'Well no, but I have been swung around by my titties!'"

At the last word, Reese looks over at me, waiting for my reaction. I just stare at him in shock, before blurting out, "What the hell was that?"

Reese raises an eyebrow at me and turns back to the road. "A joke I heard. I thought it was funny," he huffs.

"It might have been, when someone else told it!" I start chuckling, and to my surprise, so does Reese. Hearing him laugh makes the whole surreal scene even more funny to me, and I break into a cackle. That must have tickled Reese, because only a moment later, we're both laughing like madmen as we cruise through the night.

Once we pull up in front of the clubhouse and Reese cuts the truck off, he looks over at me and says, "I'm going to get some food and go to my room. Kitchen is behind the bar, anything you can scrounge up is yours." With that, he hops out and goes on in ahead of me.

There are a lot more vehicles parked outside the clubhouse than there were earlier today, so I'm apprehensive as I approach the front door. I stop for a few minutes and smoke a cigarette, trying to settle my nerves. Finally, I steel myself with the reminder that the club members already voted to allow me to prospect, and I've known most of these guys for years. I rub at my bruised eye gingerly, wishing I could see how bad it looks, then go ahead and step inside.

The door barely closes behind me before Lori swoops down on me again, wrapping me in a hug that somehow manages to rub every part of her body on me at once. "Chase, I've been waiting all afternoon to see how things went for you! Oh my god, what happened to your eye, are you okay?"

Great, I was hoping to slink off to the kitchen without anyone making a big deal of it, but Lori had to be a ditz and announce it to the entire room. "Ah, it's nothing," I hedge, trying to peel her off of me. "Just getting the hang of everything today, you know?"

"Lori!" Deacon calls from where he's sitting at the bar. "Get your tits off my prospect. Prospect, get in the kitchen and get some food!"

Lori jumps back from me as if I've caught fire, but still flashes me a flirtatious grin before skipping away. She stops at one of the pool tables and makes a show of bending over to study the game, so that her skirt climbs dangerously high up her thighs. I quickly avert my gaze, but not before I see that she isn't wearing any panties. I march stiffly to the kitchen, thankful that there are no further ambushes along the way.

Reese is already in there making a sandwich. He doesn't acknowledge me as I open the refrigerator and start digging around to see what I can find. When I emerge a moment later with a couple packages of cold cuts, Deacon is standing just behind me.

"So, how did things go out there today? Reese, did our prospect do all right?" Deacon asks him.

Reese gives a single nod, then picks up his plate and two bottles of beer. Without saying anything else, he leaves us alone in the kitchen.

"Good," Deacon says, drawing closer to take a look at my eye. "Did Reese do this to you?"

"No, this wasn't him," I tell Deacon as I begin making my sandwich. "I got this while we were doing that repossession today. Guy wasn't really happy we were there for his truck and caught me off guard."

"Well, Reese will help you with that." Deacon smiles. "He treat you all right?"

"He worked the hell out of me," I grunt. "Dude is strange, man. He's tough, though, I'll give him that. Weirdest part of the whole day was when he tried to tell me a joke."

"He told you a joke?" Deacon asks, his voice incredulous. "You must have made a good impression on him. I've only ever known him to do that if he's deep in his cups, and it's rare to see him drink much."

"You ain't missing anything, he's not very good at it." I snort. "I'm going to crash here tonight, then he's going to drive us back out to the salvage yard in the morning to get our bikes. I was too tired tonight to ride. That should tell you everything you need to know about our 'workout.'"

"I know it's been a big first day, but there's something I want to talk to you about before you call it a wrap," Deacon says. He looks around the kitchen and then peeks out into the bar area, making sure we're completely alone.

"Okay, what's on your mind?" I ask, trying to hide my confusion.

"I've got a project for you. Something has come to the club's attention, and the table decided you might be in a good position to help us investigate it. There have been a lot of young folks showing up at the hospital the last couple of months, having a bad reaction to some new drug they've taken, some pills they're getting at parties. They say it's kind of like ecstasy, but apparently, it's an opiate. It's getting its hooks into people, and we're seeing some addicts asking our distributors if they can get it for them. We don't deal in shit like this, but we haven't been able to track down who's bringing it into our town."

"All right...so how do you think I can help?" I ask him, not seeing any real connection.

"Whoever is dealing this shit is targeting young people, like I said, selling it as a party drug. You know we don't deal around schools or to teenagers. Well, whoever is slinging this shit, they don't have our scruples. I want you to keep your eyes and ears open around your school. If you see anyone passing this shit around, find out where they got it, and let us know. Now, if you get a thread, don't go tugging on it yourself. Bring it to us and we'll see where it leads, you got it?"

"Yeah, of course, that's no trouble. I always pay attention in class, you know me," I reply with a grin. "I'll just stay extra sharp, lurk around the bathrooms and smoke between classes, see what kind of stuff I see going on."

"That's good, Chase, that's really good. You get some rest and take care of yourself. Don't let anything we do interfere with your schooling, and let me know if you need anything, all right?"

"Thanks, Prez," I say. "I'll let you know immediately if I hear anything." I pick up my plate and a soda I found in the back of the fridge. Since my hands are full, Deacon walks me through the bar and punches in the code to the basement for me. I scarf down my dinner while I check out the apartment I've been assigned. Then, after a quick shower, I lie down, sleep washing over me almost instantly.

After the crazy day, my last thoughts before I drift off aren't of work or fighting, however, but of a beautiful young woman with long blonde hair, her perfect lips calling my name.

CHAPTER SIX

When I wake up the next morning, my muscles are stiffer than the sledgehammer I used to work them. I have to stand in the shower for a few minutes, letting the scalding hot water loosen me up before I can get dressed and make it upstairs. Reese is already there, standing by the bar, holding a thermos in each hand.

"Morning." I nod to him as he walks over to meet me by the front door. He hands me the thermos and goes on outside without replying. With a shrug, I follow him to the truck we brought back last night and climb into the passenger seat.

Reese doesn't say anything at all on the drive back to the salvage yard. After watching him sip at his thermos, I crack open the one he gave me to find it filled with what I think is coffee. It's so light I can't be sure, so I give it an experimental sip.

"Whew!" I say out loud. "I learned something new today. You've got a sweet tooth, man—you need to add a little coffee to this cream and sugar."

Reese lets out a derisive grunt, but other than that, we ride in silence. Once we're back at the yard, he hops out of the truck and heads straight to the office. I check my phone and see that I still have an hour until I need to be at school, so I crank up my bike and head back to my parents' house. I'm still wearing the same jeans and t-shirt from yesterday, and I want to put on something...well, not nicer, but at least cleaner before I see Sasha.

My dad, stepmom, and stepsister are still eating breakfast when I rush in the front door of their house, both of them looking up from the paper expectantly. "Chase!" My dad smiles. "How did things go yesterday? I got your text and figured you'd want to hang out with your new friends."

"It was good, Dad. I have to get changed quick and get to school!" I call to them as I head upstairs.

"Don't you at least want some food?" my dad calls after me.

"I'll take some bacon, if you've got it!" I yell down to them, my stomach rumbling in agreement.

I quickly get changed into a plain white t-shirt and some clean jeans, then throw my cut and jacket back on. As I run back down the stairs, my dad greets me at the bottom with a fat slab of bacon wedged between slices of toast.

"You guys are the best, thanks," I say as I grab the sandwich from him.

"Chase, what happened to your eye?" my dad asks me as I head back out the door.

"Don't worry, it's nothing! See you guys later!" I yell before stuffing the food in my mouth and slapping my half-helmet back onto my head. Before I can crank up the bike, I suddenly remember what else I needed here and jump back off my motorcycle to run into the garage. It only takes me a moment to find Torin's old helmet, which I strap to one of my belt loops before I fire up my bike and roar out of the driveway. I wave to my parents, who are still standing in the doorway, with slightly worried expressions on their faces.

I make record time getting to school, so intent on seeing Sasha again that I have to constantly remind myself to slow down and be cool. Being reckless on a motorcycle is dangerous, but being careless around this woman could be heart-breaking.

As I pull into the back parking lot behind the shop building, I finally have to admit to myself that the feeling in my stomach isn't from too much greasy meat this morning. I've got butterflies for this girl, and I've got them bad.

As soon as I park my bike, I see her sitting on the back steps with Mr. Aikens. He's out here, smoking his pipe and chatting with her, his normally dour face lighting up in a rare smile. I completely understand. Something about that woman makes the air around her seem warmer and it's almost intoxicating. Sasha waves to me as I take my helmet off and hang it from my handlebar, then her face breaks into a huge grin when I stand up and show her the other helmet still hanging from my belt.

She stands up and skips down the steps, jogging over to me. "You remembered!" she says breathlessly. "I suppose this means you're going to follow through and take me for a ride this afternoon?"

"If you're still up for it, absolutely. Just remember, you'll be my first, so we're going to have to take it slow..." I only realize what I've said after the words are hanging in the air between us, and I feel my cheeks begin to burn in embarrassment when she stares at me in silence.

After what seems like an eternity, she bursts into laughter, a high clear peal that is so enchanting my humiliation completely drains away. I can't help but chuckle with her, and finally say, "Maybe that didn't come out quite the way I meant it to."

"It came out perfect," she replies. "Just so you know, it will be my first time too, so I want you to be gentle."

She bursts into laughter again at my look of slack-jawed amazement, then grabs my hand and pulls me gently towards the door. "Come on, I heard Mr. Aikens tapping out his pipe. That seems to be our pre-bell warning that class is starting. Let's go mess with this Mustang and get through our day, then you can show me around your town this evening."

She starts to release my hand when we get to the sidewalk, but I shift my grip and start to intertwine my fingers with hers. She glances down at our hands before turning to me with a smile and changing her grip so our fingers link together. Hand in hand, we walk into the building, neither of us willing to let go until we have to actually get to work.

CHAPTER SEVEN

Our automotive class is over all too quickly, then the rest of the school day drags on interminably. I remember the request Deacon made of me, and I make sure to hang out in the bathrooms where the smokers are known to congregate between classes. After lunch, I wander around the back of the building, looking for any other students engaged in questionable behavior, but other than interrupting an incredibly awkward and sloppy make out session, I don't see anything noteworthy.

I'm almost exhausted by the end of the school day, from the combination of my exertions yesterday and the anticipation of spending time outside of school with Sasha. When I get back to my bike after the final bell rings, she's already there waiting for me, fiddling with the helmet I left strapped to the handlebar.

"You ready to get out of here?" I ask her as I walk up.

"I'm a little nervous," she admits. "I wanted to ask you a couple of things before we take off. I didn't mention it this morning because I wasn't sure how to ask without seeming rude."

When she trails off, I smile and say, "You want to know what happened to my face, don't you?"

"Oh my god," she gasps sarcastically. "I hadn't even noticed that! I was going to ask you what are those?" She laughs, pointing at my boots.

"Ha-ha," I say shortly, walking up to her so she can see my face clearly. "I went out last night to help with a truck repossession. The owner took exception to us towing his vehicle and knocked me upside the head."

"Well, you're lucky," Sasha says as she raises a hand to rub at my still-swollen cheek. "Most men can't pull off the brooding, bloody, tough guy look, but you wear it well. Badass, even. Now, my other question is simple: Where are you planning on running off with me today? I need to text a friend in case I'm kidnapped."

"Of course, I wouldn't imagine kidnapping you without sending out proper notifications," I say with a straight face. "Tell the search parties that they'll want to start looking for you out at the Emerald Isle boardwalk. You were most likely last seen getting funnel cakes with an extremely suspicious-looking man, who then took you for a walk out to the pier."

"That sounds like a wonderful way to go missing," Sasha gushes before holding the helmet out to me. "Now, help me get this thing on correctly."

She puts it on her head and I reach under her chin to slide the straps through the eyelets. Our faces are so close together as I work on it that I can feel her breath on my cheek, and when I cinch it tight for her, I notice her gaze lingering on my face.

"You're thinking about it too, aren't you?" she whispers teasingly as she leans into me. She steps away abruptly with a grin, then says, "Fortunately for you, I'm not the kind of girl who would take advantage of a man in such a public place."

"Then let me take us somewhere more private," I reply as I cinch up my own helmet.

She laughs and says, "Let's stick to the funnel cakes for now. Come on, see if you can get that thing running and let's get out of here."

After I crank up the bike and steady it, I wave for her to mount up behind me. I've never had a woman ride behind me on a motorcycle before, and a tingle shoots through my entire body when she throws her leg over the seat and scoots forward to press into my back. She's wearing a heavy coat, even though it's relatively warm again today, which I realize means she was planning for this moment when she got dressed. Another shiver ripples through me as her arms wind around my abdomen and she squeezes herself to me.

"Is this how I'm supposed to do it?" she asks, her breath warm in my ear.

"I don't know if it's right, but it's definitely the way I want," I reply. I kick the bike backwards out of the space, pat her hands which are clutching my midsection, then shift it into first gear. Her grip tightens into a respectable Heimlich maneuver as I putter through the parking lot, so when we come to the last stop sign before we hit the main road, I pat her hands again reassuringly.

"Squeeze as tight as you need to," I call to her. "I can take it."

"I hope so, because if the entire ride is like this, I'm going to crawl inside your coat with you!" she replies.

I chuckle at the barely-restrained fear and excitement in her voice. If I thought she was actually scared, I would stop this ride right now, but I'm pretty sure I know exactly how she's feeling. When I first got on a motorcycle, I had no idea what to expect. I remember the first time I got over thirty-five miles per hour, and how it made me feel as though I was flying. Then, I got over fifty and thought I was certainly going to sail right off the seat, my final moments nothing but a rush of vertigo followed by an abrupt and terminal impact.

You master the fear as you become accustomed to the brutal and bone-crushing pavement roaring by, inches below you, with nothing but inertia and your own sense of balance keeping you apart. You never lose respect for it though, and the exhilaration never fades.

Even with traffic, the ride out to the boardwalk only takes about twenty minutes from the school. Sasha relaxes once we get onto the main roads, and I know I've got a true convert when I hear her

71

laughter bubbling in my ear as I open the bike up on the highway. When I pull into a public beachfront parking area and kill the bike, she hops off immediately, a huge goofy grin plastered across her face.

"I love it!" she yells, as I settle the bike and dismount beside her. She throws herself at me and wraps me up in a hug. "Thank you! That was awesome. I can't wait to do this more with you!"

I stand there awkwardly for a moment before returning the hug, hyperconscious of how her breasts are pressing against me even through her coat, and the fact that this is definitely not a "brotherly hug." She's plastered to me from my neck to my knees, and when the bulge of my cock gives an appreciative twitch, she hugs me even tighter.

"You get excited riding too, don't you?" she observes as she lets me go.

"Always," I deadpan as I begin undoing my helmet. "Nothing fires me up like the rumbling of that old bike."

Sasha gets her helmet undone and hands it over to me so that I can hang it from the handlebar. "I know what you mean! That seat makes your bottom feel tingly, doesn't it?"

"Tingly?" I burst out laughing. "Yeah, I guess that's a good word for it. I've never had a girl ride with me or try to describe it before. I'll tell you one thing, though, riding always makes me thirsty. Want to get a drink and walk down to the beach with me?"

"That sounds great," Sasha agrees. She grabs my hand, making a show of lacing our fingers together, then waits for me to take the lead. "Show me around your town, Chase, and all your favorite places."

We walk hand-in-hand over to an ice cream shop at the corner. "My dad would always bring my brother and me over here when we would come to the pier and go fishing," I tell her as we go inside. "The ice cream is good, but the funnel cakes are the best. You can eat inside here too, so you don't get sand in the damned thing. I'll get one of those, what would you like?"

"I'll share whatever you're having," Sasha says. "Show me all the things you like."

I order the funnel cake and a large drink, passing Sasha the cup so she can go fill it up. "Two cups?" I ask her with a raised eyebrow.

"One." She grins, grabbing up two straws.

"My, we are getting friendly, aren't we," I comment, finally releasing her hand so she can walk over to the soda fountain.

"Not yet, but we will soon," she teases me.

Once we sit down, she sticks both the straws in the soda and we lean over it together, our noses almost touching. My mouth is incredibly dry, partly from riding but mostly from the woman in front of me. I take a long pull on the straw, noticing at the last instant that Sasha isn't drinking, but is instead grinning devilishly. I find out why an instant later, when the strangest mix of flavors I've ever tasted washes out my mouth.

I jerk back from the straw with my lips puckered, while Sasha bursts out laughing. "Man, I think they need to change the cartridge, that tastes awful!" I snort. "What did you put in there?"

"Everything!" Sasha giggles. "I like to mix them up, so I hit the root beer, the coke, even the tea!"

"Even the *tea*? You heathen, no one pollutes a southern gentleman's tea! I call shenanigans too, you didn't sip that mess. You don't really drink mess like that!"

"*Shenanigans!*" Sasha's giggles turn into a peal of laughter. "Oh my god, that's hilarious. Have you seen *Super Troopers?*"

"Not in a while," I reply, as I get up to go dump out the mess she created in our cup. "Let's watch it together some time. I love that movie."

When I get back to the table with a normal beverage, Sasha is already peeling off the crusty edges of our funnel cake. "I like that idea," she tells me. "Smart of you to go ahead and plan our next date too. If something happens and this one goes sour, you've already got a contingency plan."

I pick up the funnel cake and take a huge bite. "A smart man always plans several steps ahead," I tell her seriously after I swallow. Or as seriously as I can, with powdered sugar covering half my face.

After we finish off the cake, we stick our straws back in the cup, foreheads touching as we actually finish off the drink this time. We clasp hands again on our way out the door and stay glued together for the next hour as we walk around the boardwalk. I show her the arcade I spent a lot of time in growing up, and she insists on dragging us inside to play skee-ball. Once we've burned through all my change, we head back outside.

"Over here is the tattoo parlor where a lot of the guys in the club get their ink," I tell her as we pass by the shop, brightly-lit with all manner of flashing neon signs.

"I want to get a tattoo!" Sasha blurts out.

"Ha!" I snort. "What are you thinking about getting, a butterfly? Maybe...oh, god forbid, maybe a tramp stamp?"

She smacks me in the chest with her free hand. "What kind of girl do you think I am? A *tramp stamp*? That's a terrible term! Lower back tattoos can be sexy. But no, I would get something meaningful, something important to me. I don't know what exactly, but it would have to be special."

"Well, when you think of what you want, you let me know. I'll bring you myself," I promise her. "I'm going to be here soon enough. I've got a design for a sleeve I want to get done." I motion to my right arm with the hand she's clasping.

"God, that would be sexy," she practically purrs at me, leaning in to press herself against me. "I want to come with you when you get inked, maybe get some ideas for something I would like done. I want to see how a big tough guy like you handles the needle too!"

"It shouldn't be too bad," I tell her. "It'll probably be rough around my elbow, but the upper arm and forearm are meaty. My back is going to be rough, they'll be going across the spine and some rib areas, I've heard those are unpleasant."

"Who do you know with back tattoos?" she asks.

"All the members of my MC have the Savage Kings' emblem on their back. Once I'm patched in, I'll be getting it too. It's a rite of passage. I'm excited about it. The club isn't just a hobby. Being a brother in the MC is going to set me up for life," I explain.

"Set you up for life? You going to be a 'made man,' like the Godfather or something like that?" She grins at me.

"Eh, not quite like that. The MC owns some businesses in the area, and my brother Torin is already talking about expanding our holdings when he gets back from the Army. Like this tattoo shop, for example. Torin told me he'd like for the club to own our shop, maybe even recruit a brother who is really good at ink to do all of our art for us. Those shops are damn good earners too."

"So, what would you be doing to 'earn' once you're a member? Do you have a job with this club?"

"Nah, I'm still learning the ropes right now. Yesterday, I went out on a repossession. They'll probably have me doing that for a while. Besides the towing and scrapyard the club runs, there's an auto shop where we work on cars and bikes. The MC used to make money doing some racing when Fast Eddie was younger, but he's too old and beat up to drag race bikes anymore."

"Drag racing? I would love to see that! Do they still do it around here?"

"Yeah," I confirm. "We do some bike modifications for some local racers, and they hold exhibitions every few months. That's another date we can plan, how about that?"

"I love it," Sasha agrees. "You can ink that into your calendar for us too. Now, where are we headed next?"

"Let's walk out on the pier," I tell her, pulling her in that direction. We're close by, and as I lead her through the front doors, she pauses to read the sign detailing the fees.

"It says we need five bucks just to walk out there and hang out." She sighs. "I always thought that was a rip-off! You bought the cake, so I'll pay for this," she offers.

"No need," I reassure her. I nod to the young guy at the register, jerking a thumb over my shoulder and turning to show him my cut. He gives me a nod and waves us on past.

"Oh, I see how it is," Sasha grins. "You tough guy bikers get preferential treatment, just get to walk right on by if you don't cause any trouble?"

"No." I laugh. "The club owns this pier. My Uncle Deacon bought it after a hurricane blew through back in the eighties, and tore it up. He had it rebuilt. These places make good money off of tourists. Seriously, the club has all sorts of ways to earn money. They'll find a good spot for me once I've learned all the ins and outs of their businesses."

"You're not going to end up riding a register at the pier, are you? Something tells me you might be a little off-putting to some of the tourists." She laughs.

"Hey, that's rough! You think I would scare away the fishermen?" I joke. "Nah, don't worry, club brothers don't do that sort of menial labor. They actually hire locals to help with that sort of thing. I'll be doing more...respectable work. Yeah, that's a good word for it, respectable."

As we're talking, we walk the length of the pier, passing by a few fishermen idly checking their lines. Nothing seems to be biting, except for one unlucky old fellow who hauls in a stingray just after we pass him. Once we're out at the end of the pier, Sasha unzips the jacket she has been wearing and stands facing the ocean as the chilly breeze ruffles her long blonde hair.

I can't resist raising a hand to touch it as it floats around her shoulders, winding a thread of her thick golden waves around my finger. She turns to me with a smile and places a hand on my chest, before her other arm slides under my cut and around my back, gripping my t-shirt and pulling me closer to her.

"It's beautiful out here," she comments as she snuggles her head into my chest, still looking out over the ocean.

"I've always loved the coast," I reply, looking down and still playing with the curl of her hair. "But I think I've found something even more beautiful out here."

The two of us go quiet as I try to soak up every detail of this day, committing the sweet flavor of funnel cake on my lips, the salty smell of the ocean, and Sasha's warmth pressed against me all to my memory. In just a few days, everything in my life seems to be changing in the best way. I hesitate with whether or not I should tell her what I'm thinking right this second. If it were anyone else, I'd probably keep my mouth shut. But Sasha is...different, so I ask her, "Have you ever had a moment where you get a feeling...where you know nothing in your life is ever going to be the same?"

"I think I'm about to," Sasha whispers as she turns her head up to me, the longing in her eyes telling me she feels the same as I do.

I only have to bend down slightly for our lips to meet for the first time, her soft moan filling my mouth as she pulls me to her. My hand that had been twirling her hair slips to the back of her neck, the two of us struggling to draw even closer together. As the kiss grows more passionate, our tongues seek each other out, the next few minutes of pure bliss sealing us together in ways that I somehow knew would affect the course of our lives.

When we finally part, both of us flustered and breathless, a series of splashes and chirps draw our eyes to the water below us. "Dolphins!" Sasha cries, pulling me to her and leaning both of us over the rail to get a better view. A pod of the beautiful creatures leaps and calls out just below us at the end of the pier, almost seeming to cheer and celebrate for the two of us.

"I think they want to see more," I comment, as I use my hand on the back of Sasha's neck to gently pull her attention back to me.

"Well, let's make sure our encore is memorable for them," she whispers as she pushes me against the rail, pressing herself into me and grabbing my face in both of her hands to kiss me.

I'm not sure how long we would have stayed out there, if Sasha's cell phone hadn't started buzzing. My hand finds its way into her back pocket, lingering longer than is absolutely necessary on her bottom, before sliding her phone out and handing it to her as she steps away from me.

"Hi, Mom," Sasha says as she answers, out of breath. She cups her hand around the phone, trying to cover it as much as possible from the wind. "Sure, put a plate in the microwave for me, and I'll be back home later. Okay, thanks, Mom. Love you!"

"I guess I'll need to get you back soon," I tell her, unable to hide the regret in my voice.

"Don't worry, Chase. Remember we already scheduled quite a few future adventures. When do you want to get back together and hang out? After school again sometime this week, or maybe this weekend?"

We start walking back down the pier, our hands automatically seeking each other out. "I have some club business tomorrow afternoon, but if they stick to the same schedule, I'll have every other day off. Let me check tomorrow, and then we can figure it out. Sound good?"

"Sounds good," Sasha agrees.

"Do you want me to take you back to your house, or should we head back to school?"

"Drop me off back at the school. My dad is letting me drive one of the used cars from his lot until my Mustang is ready. I'll round it up and then head home."

We make it back to my motorcycle, and get our helmets on, with only a brief break for more kissing. Once Sasha is secure behind me, we ride back to the school. The sun is starting to set, the early evening sky painted in streaks of purple, red, and orange. It's the most beautiful sunset I've ever seen, and I know I feel that way because of the woman riding with me.

Sasha points out the car she's using once we're back in the school parking lot, though I probably could have guessed which one was hers. It's a newer model Mustang, and one of the last vehicles left on the lot. Once I park beside it, we get off the bike, both of us moving slower as the time for us to separate draws closer.

"Before I go," Sasha says, as she hands me her helmet, "there's one more thing I wanted to ask you."

"Shoot," I reply. "Anything you want to know. For you, I'm an open book."

"You mentioned this morning that you stayed out at your MC's clubhouse last night. This is probably stupid, but...are there a lot of women that hang out there?"

Before I can answer, she holds up a hand to stop me. "Wait," she continues. "Let me rephrase the question. I don't actually care if there are women at your clubhouse. What I want to know, Chase Fury, is how many girls are you currently seeing? This thing between us feels...it's special, something I haven't felt before. If you're playing around, or..."

"Stop," I tell her gently, as I put her helmet down and grab her hands. "I get it. The motorcycle, the club, the lifestyle, of course you're worried. Yes, there are women who hang out around the clubhouse, trying to hook up with the guys. You don't have to worry about them. I'm not seeing anyone else. I'm not interested in anyone else. I had a feeling as soon as I saw you, a feeling that turned into a certainty once I got to spend time with you. Sasha, whatever this is between us...I want it. No, I need it. I have to have it. I mean, just the thought of you leaving now makes me feel like I..."

"Makes it kind of hard to breathe," Sasha finishes.

"Exactly," I confirm as I wrap her up in a hug. "I've never felt like this with anyone. I can't stand to leave, and I can't wait for tomorrow to come so we can see each other again. But look, I know you have to get home, so just remember...if you want me, I'm yours."

"Does this mean I can call you my boyfriend? You and me, no one else?"

"You're damn right, Sasha. You and me, no one else. Now, get yourself home before you get grounded or something. I'll see you in the morning."

"Thanks for today, Chase. See you tomorrow!" Sasha waves as she walks around her car and climbs in. I crouch down by the passenger side to watch her, then wave as she begins to drive away.

Once she's out of the lot, I finally get back on my bike, suddenly feeling exhausted after all the excitement of the last two days.

Before I leave, I pull out a cigarette and sit on my motorcycle, thinking over our date and trying to decide where to go for the night. I already love the clubhouse, but I haven't brought any of my clothes there yet and know my parents are worried about me. I decide to head on back to their house to spend some time with them and reassure them that everything is going well.

Besides, I want to tell someone, anyone, about Sasha.

I thought Deacon offering me my cut was the best thing that had ever happened to me. I had no idea, just a short time later, I would meet a woman who would mean even more to me.

CHAPTER EIGHT

The next few weeks pass by in a blur, flashes of backbreaking labor and exhausting workouts interspersed with blissful days filled with Sasha's presence. Every moment I wasn't working for the club or training with Reese, she and I were together. We met each other's parents, mine seeming much happier about the relationship than hers, ate dinner at one another's houses, studied together, and only parted ways when the nights drove us apart. Though it took every bit of my willpower, I respected her too much to push our physical relationship too quickly. Sasha confided in me early on that she was a virgin, and I was determined that I would wait until hell froze over, or until we got married, if that was what she wanted.

The unusual streak of warm weather in January that allowed me to ride my motorcycle only lasted a week, but by that time, Sasha was already coming over to my house in the mornings to pick me up. I would have driven my truck to her house, but since I was on her way and the car she was borrowing from her dad's dealership was much nicer, she insisted on taking us to school. Riding with her was one of my favorite parts of the day. We had a chance to play all the music that was close to our hearts, showing each other what we enjoyed, and engage in frequent hot and heavy make out sessions that left the windows fogged over.

Our automotive technology class went to work on Sasha's Mustang with an almost religious passion. By the second week of February, the last coat of red paint was dry, and on the twelfth of the month, Mr. Aikens gathered our class together and pronounced that we would all be getting an A for the semester, due to the exemplary work that had been displayed.

"Thanks for driving me to school today," Sasha says to me as we stand together in the parking lot after school by her newly restored cherry-red Mustang.

"You don't have to thank me for that, sweetheart. Hell, there have been a lot of country songs written about getting girls like you into a pickup truck."

"You know any songs about girls in hot rods picking up bikers?" Sasha asks with a smile.

"When people see us together, one will get written, watch and see."

"I'm so glad it got finished before Valentine's Day. You have club stuff tomorrow, but we're still on for Thursday night, right?" she asks.

"Of course we're on. It's our first Valentine's Day together. The guys know better than to screw with me over something this important. I'll make sure not to do anything to get my face marked up before Thursday too." I chuckle.

"I wasn't sure about this 'training' they were putting you through when you first showed up with that knot on your head," Sasha says as she wraps her arms around me. "But whatever they're feeding you or making you do is paying off. You were always hard and hot Mr. Fury, but you've turned it up a notch."

"Yeah, I've gained like ten pounds of muscle or something in the last five weeks. That guy Reese I told you about has been making me drink some crap he mixes up in the blender."

"He's not giving you steroids, is he? I would hate to think he's giving you something that's going to shrink your balls or have some other weird side effect."

"My balls are just fine, thank you very much!" I laugh at her. "I'll even let you check them sometime, if you're so concerned. Don't worry, he drinks the stuff too, he's not doing anything harmful to me. It's just protein powder, I think."

"Well, whatever it is, I like the results," she says, as she lifts up the bottom of the black hoodie I'm wearing under my cut, sliding a hand over my abs. With a grin, she leans up and whispers in my ear, "I want to see just how far these ridges run."

I tighten my embrace around her, catching her lips in a kiss. We stay locked together for a few moments, before Sasha pulls away, smiling.

"Save it for our date Thursday," she says. "I'm driving, but you'll be the navigator. Where are you planning on taking us that night?"

"I made some calls and got us reservations over at *Vincenzo's*," I reply.

"What! My dad tried to get a reservation there, he wanted to take my mom. They said they were booked up, like, six months ago! How did you manage that?"

"Hey, you've been here long enough to see how things work. In this town, there's always somebody that owes the club a favor. It was no big deal, I just called and let them know who I was, and a table magically appeared."

"Oh, this is going to be great! I've got the perfect dress I want to wear, and you, Mr. Fury, well...I can't wait to see you all dressed up. What do you think we should do about gifts for each other?" Sasha asks me. "I've got some ideas, but I want to know what you're thinking."

"Ah, well, I kind of already got yours arranged," I hedge. "I didn't think the car would be ready today. I was kind of hoping they could hold it until Thursday, but..."

"Hold my car until Thursday?" Sasha asked in mock outrage. "Why? What did you do to my baby, Chase Fury?"

"Just climb in, I'll show you," I tell her with a chuckle. Mr. Aikens had pulled the car out of the garage, so she hadn't yet sat down inside of it today to see the latest addition I wired into it over the weekend.

"Oh shit, Chase, this is awesome!" Sasha gushes once she's in the driver's seat. She runs her hands over the face of the new Pioneer CD player I had installed.

"That old factory radio you had in this thing was busted, and I know how hard you rock," I tell her as I plop down into the passenger seat. "You already had new speakers when you brought the car in, so I just finished the upgrade."

Sasha puts the key in the ignition and turns on the power without cranking the car. When the radio lights up and the display reads "Sirius," she leans over and kisses me on the cheek.

"It's got satellite radio too! Did a subscription come with the receiver, or...?"

"Nah," I interject when she leaves the question hanging. "I paid for a lifetime subscription. A car like this is something you keep for life, and I didn't want you to have to worry about payments for radio service."

"Chase!" Sasha protests. "That's crazy! How much did all that cost? You goofball, I was talking about exchanging cards, maybe taking a road trip together!"

"You needed it to make the Mustang complete," I tell her. "Once I got to know you, this project was a labor of love for both of us. It had to be perfect. You don't have to go crazy buying me things to try to even us up. We don't have to one-up each other."

"Thank you," Sasha says simply, leaning over to kiss me again, on the lips this time.

"Now, crank this monster up and take off, baby. I have to get to work, they're sending me out on my own with the tow truck today. I've been making good money working with the club already, so we'll have a big time Thursday night."

"Call me when you get done tonight!" Sasha calls to me as I get out of the car.

"I will, sweetheart, see you later." I grin. I close the door and back away as Sasha cranks the Mustang, the thunder of her huge engine drowning out even the roar my Harley normally makes. With a final wave, she rumbles away, the sound of the car hanging in the air long after it's actually out of view.

I walk back over to my truck, wishing the weather would warm up again so I could get my bike out of the garage. I don't mind the old beat-up pickup I bought off my dad, but it just doesn't feel like an extension of me the way my motorcycle does. I'm not sure any car would, honestly. The Mustang suits Sasha, its power and grace, a fitting carriage for a woman like her. This dusty old truck doesn't share my "character." I sit down inside of it, then light a cigarette and relax a moment before I head off to work.

I'm daydreaming about cars that might somehow better suit me, so I don't notice when my friend Robbie approaches from behind the truck. I give a startled jerk when he knocks on the window, which I have cracked to let out the smoke.

"Hey, man," I say as I roll down the window the rest of the way. "What's going on? I was just getting ready to head out. You need a ride?"

"No thanks, Chase, nothing like that. I just wanted to run something by you," Robbie tells me.

"Okay, shoot. What's on your mind, man?"

Robbie leans in conspiratorially, crossing his arms on the windowsill before he whispers, "That girl April I've been seeing wanted to see if I could get some weed, you know, get smoked up for Valentine's Day. You got anything I could buy off you?"

"Ha! Smoked up for Valentine's, huh?" I laugh. "I'm not holding anything right now, man, sorry. Sounds like it could be a romantic evening if you can find a hook-up."

"Yeah, I'm hoping it could put her in the proper mood, you

know." Robbie sighs. "I thought you can get stuff sometimes from the club, and was hoping..."

I interrupt him before he can ask anything further of me. "I know, man, but I'm not a dealer. I get a little bit now and then, when I'm going to a party or hanging out, but I don't just carry it around. You know how it is, man, it's not something you want to have in your pocket around here day to day. Ask around though, one of the boys in the shop will help you out."

"Yeah, thanks, Chase," Robbie says. "Take it easy, man, I'll see you tomorrow."

Once Robbie wanders off, I roll up the window and crank the engine, knowing it's time for me to head out to the garage. I make a mental note to check with Robbie again later this week, though, and see if he had any luck finding a supply. The MC frowns on anyone in this town slinging any sort of drugs around school, but if Deacon's suspicions are correct, Robbie might actually find a dealer willing to work with him. Everyone knows from my cut who I'm with, so getting information about any activity the club doesn't approve of can be difficult. My boy Robbie might accidentally stumble onto the lead I need.

CHAPTER NINE

I don't usually smoke very much, but on Valentine's Day, I go through half a pack throughout the course of the day. Once I get home after school, I lock my cigarettes in my desk drawer in my room before taking a shower, determined not to have that smell hanging over me when Sasha comes to pick me up.

She had insisted on driving for our date tonight. I couldn't really blame her—that Mustang is one of the most badass vehicles in Emerald Isle. As the time for her to arrive approaches, I pace around the long front porch of my parents' farmhouse, trying to figure out why I'm so edgy today.

"It's this damn suit," I mumble to myself, pulling at the collar of the fresh white shirt still warm from ironing.

"That's hardly a suit," Jade, my stepsister, says from the porch swing, where she's painting her toenails. "I don't even know what to call that. Biker formal?"

"I'm going on a date, not to a funeral." I snort. She's right, though. I'm wearing a white dress shirt tucked into a new pair of jeans, and I put on a black tie and buttoned my cut. I even shined my boots until the leather gleamed.

"You don't look bad," Jade admits. "It's just not a suit. You'd really be miserable with the proper pants and coat. Does Sasha know what you're wearing?"

"Sasha knows what I always wear," I tell her as I plop down on the swing beside her. Jade flashes me a look of annoyance as my weight shifts the swing, making her paint go awry.

"You're getting fat," she chides me.

"I am not getting fat!" I protest, then unbutton the cuffs of my shirt and roll the sleeves up to my elbows. I hold my arm out and make a fist, flexing the muscles in my forearm. "See that? Does that look like fat to you?"

"Well, you're getting bigger, fast," she concedes. "Whenever you're home for dinner, you eat more than the rest of the house combined. You can understand my confusion, I'm sure."

Before I have a chance to respond, I hear the monstrous growling of Sasha's Mustang as she downshifts and pulls into our driveway. A moment later, the car comes into view. Jade's jaw drops open as she watches it pull up to the front of the house.

I have to remind myself to close my mouth too, and take a deep steadying breath when Sasha steps out of the car. She's wearing a short and very tight black dress, the thin shoulder straps stressed almost to breaking by the weight of her breasts. She takes a moment by the car to pull on a pair of heels, as she prefers to drive barefoot.

"What God did you pray to for her?" Jade whispers. "Or what did you pay the devil? Jesus, Chase, she's built like that and has a hot rod *too*?"

"Why are you acting so surprised? Sasha's been hanging around for weeks, you're acting like this is the first time you've seen her!"

"It's the first time I've seen her like *that*!" Jade replies.

"Don't be jealous." I grin to my little sister. "I'm sure your prayers will be answered someday, if you keep acting right."

"You've never acted right a day in your life," Jade scoffs.

"Hey guys!" Sasha says, as she steps onto the porch.

I'm already on my feet, walking over to wrap my arms around her waist. "You look amazing," I say, bending down to place a light kiss on her lips.

"Oh, you're respecting the lipstick." She smiles. "You can smudge it a bit if you want, I've got more."

I kiss her again, this time more fiercely as she presses herself into me. She shifts and pushes me gently against the porch railing, her arms snaking around my neck. "Okay, well"—Jade coughs—"you two have a great night. I'm going to go forget I ever saw this."

"That's probably best," I tell her as I come up for air.

"Good night, Jade," Sasha says with a blush.

After my stepsister goes inside, Sasha steps back and brushes her hands over my leather cut. "You look sharp, I like it. You ready to head out to the restaurant?"

"Hell yeah, I'm starving," I reply. "Take me for a ride tonight, and let's see how you handle that beast."

"Oh, I intend to," she says with a coy smile, grabbing my hand and leading me down the steps to the Mustang. She insists on opening the passenger side door for me and making sure I'm in before coming around and kicking off her shoes. "Hold these for me," she orders as she places the heels in my lap.

She cranks the car up and gets us down to the end of the driveway, pausing to check for any oncoming traffic. I haven't been able to look away from her since she sat down, entranced by the way her already short dress rides up her thighs as she works the clutch, and mesmerized by the way her heavy breasts sway and strain against their thin fabric cage.

"Are you wearing a bra?" I blurt out without thinking, feeling my face burn as soon as the question leaves my mouth.

Sasha drops the car into neutral and sets the brake, then twists in her seat to face me. Grinning and holding eye contact, she reaches up and slowly lowers the strap on her left shoulder, pulling her arm through and freeing her breast. "No, Chase, as you can see, I'm not. Just these," she adds, as she slowly peels off what looks like a flower sticker over her nipple. "Pasties. Very tasteful, don't you think?"

I swear, it feels like my eyes are going to bulge from my head trying to take in how sexy she is, sitting there holding her breast, almost in offering to me. I practically lunge at her, my hand cupping her as our mouths crash together. She giggles softly as her foot accidentally hits the accelerator, the engine revving in mockery of our passion. She mimics a low growling of her own as my mouth dives down to her breast, seeking out her exposed nipple and ravishing it with my tongue.

"Fuck, Sasha, you're...you're perfect. I mean..." I say, as I gasp for breath while sucking and lightly nipping at her breast. I drop my hand to reach down and cup her ass, beginning to drag her out of her seat and over to me.

"We should probably take it down a notch, just for now," Sasha gasps and laughs. "We're going to miss dinner, and your parents are eventually going to come check to see if we're having car trouble."

"Oh shit, we're still in the driveway?" I grin at her. "I thought I was halfway to paradise."

"You are," Sasha whispers as she straightens her dress and puts her pasty back in place. She gets the strap of her dress back up and then actually bounces in her seat, trying to settle her tits back into the bodice. "Well, I've worked up quite an appetite. Let's hit the road! Navigator, which way?"

I point off to the left and Sasha drops the car into gear. I'm still staring at her, and from the small smile on her face, I know she doesn't mind. As soon as she runs the gears and we're on the main road, I reach over to place my hand on her thigh, teasing the hem of her dress up a little farther.

"I'm surprised you haven't asked yet, Chase," she says, as she turns down the stereo.

"Oh? Asked what?" I say absently, still watching my hand as it rubs gently at her smooth thigh.

"If I'm wearing panties." She grins over at me.

The damned woman did it to me again. She bursts into a peal of laughter at my look of shock, then places her hand on top of mine as I start to draw back a bit.

"Your face." She giggles. "Oh my god, Chase, you're hilarious. My big bad biker gets flustered so easily, and it's so much fun!"

"Well..." I drawl as I regain my composure, my hand gripping her thigh more firmly. "Since the question has been asked, what's the answer?"

"There's only one way to find out, isn't there?" Sasha replies, letting go of my hand to place it back with her other on the steering wheel.

That's all the invitation I need. I shift in my seat to change hands, placing my right one on her thigh and sliding it up, pausing to use my thumb to hook the hem of her dress. Sasha shifts in her seat to accommodate me, and as my hand explores the smooth expanse of her hip, then her lower belly, it quickly becomes apparent that she is indeed wearing nothing underneath.

Sasha's lips part, and she gasps slightly as my fingers find a thin strip of soft hair which I gently rub, stroking downward until I feel the heat radiating from her. My index finger easily finds her clit, and I begin to rub it in small slow circles as she continues to focus on the road ahead.

"Turn right at the next light," I order, never stopping the motion of the single finger pressing into her most sensitive area.

"Uh-hmmm," she agrees in a soft moan, still keeping her eyes ahead.

"I can't tell you how impressed I am, sweetheart. Sneaking out of the house with no panties to tease your boyfriend," I tell her as my finger continues its dance.

"I had panties on when I left." Sasha grins. "They're in the console. I knew they'd be soaked before I got to your house. Oh, oh God, Chase," Sasha moans as a tremor begins in her thighs and her belly tightens. She shifts forward in her seat, trapping my hand under her, then rocks back and forth to grind against my finger still caressing her.

"Right there," she gasps as we roll up to the stoplight, the car coming to an abrupt halt as Sasha puts a bit too much pressure on the pedal. "Fuck! Fuck! Fuck!" Sasha cries, as she rocks violently back and forth on my hand, then suddenly leans back in her seat with a long, content sigh. She shifts the car down into first gear, and as I pull my hand back, we continue right down the road.

"It's on the left up here," I say as I point out the window. Sasha's gaze follows where I'm pointing, then she bursts into another gale of laughter.

"You just finger blasted my pussy and the first thing you say is, 'it's on the left up here.'" Sasha giggles. "Oh man, you're the best, Chase. This is going to be the greatest night ever."

"For both of us, sweetheart?" I tease, raising an eyebrow at her.

"Oh yes, baby, for both of us," Sasha agrees as she pulls into the parking lot. "You can count on that."

Sasha gets out of the car and takes a moment to get her shoes on and her dress straightened. When she turns to me, her cheeks are still glowing, and the smile she hits me with is so dazzling I simply stand, awestruck, staring at her until she hooks her arm in mine and starts walking towards the front door of the restaurant.

"That's a very durable dress," I tell her as I hold the door open.

"Durable, huh? That wasn't the look I was going for tonight, but thank you," she replies with a roll of her eyes.

"I mean, you look drop dead gorgeous in it, sweetheart. I'm just saying that it's taken a lot of punishment already and it still looks pristine."

"We'll have to test its limits later," Sasha whispers into my ear as we approach the hostess. "I'm hopeful it won't survive the night."

After giving the hostess my name, we're seated immediately at a small private booth. The lights are dimmed tonight, giving the entire venue a soft, romantic light.

"This place is perfect, Chase. Thank you for bringing me here," Sasha says, as she reaches across the table to take my hand.

"Wait till you try their food. Best Italian joint in the area, hands down. My stepsister says their cheesecake is really good too, but I never had a taste for it."

"Cheesecake? Oh no, I'm going to eat too much and be so miserable later," Sasha pouts.

"I'm sure I can find some ways to help you get some relief," I tell her with a wink.

CHAPTER TEN

For the next hour, Sasha and I indulge ourselves in pasta nirvana. Reese has been encouraging me to eat as much as possible after the grueling workouts I've endured, so I take the opportunity tonight to load up on my favorites. Sasha doesn't go as crazy as I do, but when she finishes the fettucine she ordered, she does reach her fork over to my side to steal a few bites of my manicotti and my eggplant parmesan.

"Oof," she groans as she finally lays down her fork in surrender. "I give up, Chase. I wanted to try a little bit of everything, but there is no way to keep up. Everything here is wonderful, and I can't handle anymore."

"The best way to try everything is repeat visits. I'll make sure to bring you back more often so you get a shot at everything." I drag a crust of bread around my dish to soak up some sauce, then finish it off. "So, you ready for that cheesecake?"

She laughs. "There is no way in hell I'm going to fit anything else in tonight."

"You sure you didn't save any room at all?" I ask, while reaching under the table to place a hand on her knee.

Sasha grins at that and says, "There's always room for..." before trailing off when our server appears.

"Can I get you two anything else?" she asks.

"We're ready for the check, please," Sasha replies, a flush rising in her cheeks.

"Perfect, I'll take this when you're ready," the server says, pulling a thin black book from her apron and laying it down on the table.

Sasha grabs it before I can get my hand out from under the table, spinning it towards herself and flipping it open. Her eyes bulge in shock as her gaze scrolls down to the totals at the bottom of the page. "Holy shit, Chase, you should have told me how expensive this was going to be! You didn't have to bring me here, we could have gone to an Applebee's or something!"

I reach inside my cut and unzip the pocket in the inner lining, then draw out a tightly-rolled wad of money. "I like this place," I reassure her. "And I wanted to introduce you to it. I'll be bringing you here again, believe me. The money isn't an issue."

Sasha just watches me for a moment as I deftly unwrap the rubber band from around the roll of cash, then begin peeling off one hundred-dollar bills. I place three of them with the bill, then slide it to the edge of the table before re-wrapping and tucking the cash back into my cut.

"Rubber band banking, huh? If I didn't think you were a biker boy before, I definitely would now. Jesus, Chase, how much was that?" Sasha asks me.

"Few grand," I reply nonchalantly, even though I know damn well it's more money than I've ever had in my hand at once in my entire life.

"When we met at the beginning of the school year, you were having to scavenge bike parts out at the scrapyard, and now you've got enough to buy one straight-out in your pocket! You know, I'm starting to think I'm a good influence on you. You've really come up in the world since you started hanging around me," Sasha says.

"It's definitely you." I laugh. "What can I say? You drive a man to perform his best. Truth, though? At the end of January, my Uncle Deacon came to me with my share of the monthly earnings. The club did good business over the New Year, so everyone got a little extra in their cut." My cell phone begins to buzz in my pocket, but I reach down and silence it without giving it a second thought.

"You were serious about the club being a job, not just a hobby or lifestyle," Sasha observes. "I'm glad, Chase. I've already seen how happy it makes you. Being able to make a living doing something you enjoy, with people you like, that's honestly priceless."

"Yeah it is." I let out a pleased sigh as I sink back into the booth. "How do you think you'll make out after college, if you go into journalism? Any money to be made there?"

Sasha had told me her dream was to be a reporter, maybe even on the international stage, but I had no idea if that was something that could pay the bills. My cell phone buzzes again, but I silence it just as quickly as before.

"It just depends on how good I am at it," she replies. "You see the newscasters and reporters from your local channels shopping in the same grocery stores we do, their kids going to the same public schools, so it's not like they're making biker bankrolls," she adds, rolling her eyes. "I expect I'll make enough to get by, though."

"Well, you won't have to worry about supporting me," I tell her as the server picks up the cash.

"Keep the change." I wave to the server as she begins to walk away, before continuing to speak to Sasha. "Whatever you want to do in your life, you do it. I'll have your back every step of the way, for as long as you'll have me around. I mean it, sweetheart."

"Chase..." Sasha trails off, her eyes filled with emotion as she takes my hand. "Thank you. You have to know, I..."

My cell phone buzzes again, and Sasha has noticed the sound the vibrations are making. Whatever she was going to say trails off as she glances down towards my pocket under the table. She lets go of my hand with a sigh.

"You better check that, it might be something important," she says.

"Shit," I mutter, hating that our moment was interrupted. I dig out my phone, ready to raise hell with whoever had derailed our date. As soon as I get it out, my stomach churns unpleasantly. The caller I.D. shows "Kings Clubhouse," the name I entered when I punched their main line into my phone.

"This is Chase," I say by way of greeting when I answer.

"You've created a problem for us," the voice on the line tells me.

"Reese?" I ask, trying to verify who the voice belongs to.

"Do you know a boy named Robbie Jordan?" the voice I think is Reese asks.

"Yeah, why?"

"He's in our clubhouse with a girl who appears to be dying. He's asking for you. Here," the voice tells me as the phone is passed. At least I can be pretty sure it was Reese. He's the only one at the clubhouse who talks to me that way.

"Chase, you there?" Robbie gasps as he takes the phone.

"Yeah, man. What the hell is going on, why are you out at the clubhouse? They said you had someone injured with you?"

"No, Chase, listen! Remember I asked you about getting some weed? I did what you said and got some stuff from this other dude at school, some pills and shit, but when April took it, she started having a seizure or something, man!"

"Wait, Robbie, what the fuck?" I interrupt him. "Why the fuck did you bring her to the clubhouse? Call an ambulance or something!"

"My phone was dead, and we were out here near the place. You were the first person I thought of, man! Shit, our parents can't find out about this! I thought, maybe if she got a drink, a Coke or something, we could see if it passed..." Robbie's voice breaks and I realize he's crying, right on the verge of becoming hysterical.

"Robbie, get it together, man. What did you take, exactly? Do you know what it was? Who did you buy it from?" I ask him, trying to keep my voice level to calm him down.

"I asked a couple of people who couldn't help me, but then that dude, Brian Lehmann, found me and told me he could hook me up. You know, Bald Brian? I thought the dude was just some straight-edger, but he said he had a connection. I got these pills from him, man, and he said it would be a good time, but..."

"Brian Lehmann? Robbie, Brian's not some straight-edger, he's a fucking skinhead!" I cover my mouth to try to keep my voice down, as I can feel my anger rising. Sasha leans closer to me across the table, looking shocked.

"I don't...what?" Robbie asks in confusion. "What do you mean, like a Nazi?"

"Yes, like a goddamn Nazi. He runs around with the Aryans. Christ, Robbie, he got expelled last year, don't you remember?"

"I thought they let him back into school. I mean, I see him down the road at the gas station all the time..."

"Put Reese back on the phone," I order Robbie. "Go check on April."

"Oh shit, April..." I hear as Robbie's voice trails away, before the phone is picked back up.

"Reese, is that you?" I ask. Instead of an answer, I hear a wailing cry in the background from the clubhouse.

"Reese, are you there? What the hell was that?" I demand.

"The girl died," Reese says tonelessly.

"She...oh fuck, no, no, no. Reese, did you..." I begin to ask.

"Deacon has called the law," Reese interrupts. "Did Robbie tell you anything?"

"Yeah, yeah, he told me he bought some drugs out at the school from a dude who runs with the Aryans, guy named Brian Lehmann. He's a kid who got expelled from our school last year..."

"That's enough," Reese interrupts me again. "I can find him. We need you here, Prospect."

I know by the way he says my title, it's a command, not a request. "I'm on my way," I reply, but the line is already dead.

"I heard part of it," Sasha says, as I close the phone. "Except for the last bit. Where are we going?"

I get up from the booth and help Sasha to her feet. "I'm sorry, sweetheart. I'll tell you everything in the car. I need you to get me to the clubhouse, fast."

Sasha's eyebrows draw down as her forehead crinkles in irritation, but she takes my hand and we leave the restaurant quickly. We jump into the car, Sasha not even caring that her dress rides up, and as soon as she kicks off her shoes, the engine roars to life. As she peels out of the parking lot, I tell her everything I know from the phone call.

"They said April Neil is dead?" Sasha gasps. "It was some sort of drug reaction?"

"The club asked me to keep my eyes open for anyone slinging shit around the school," I explain. "Someone in the area has been pushing some new drug that's been causing bad reactions. They've been selling to high schoolers and college kids, primarily. Robbie told me who he got it from, so if nothing else, at least we've got a lead. The Savage Kings don't allow shit like this in Emerald Isle. *Ever*. It's one of the reasons we get a pass from the locals on so many other things."

"But what do they need you there for? Just because of Robbie, or are they planning something?"

Sasha sounds worried, and I try to think of something to say to reassure her. I can't, though, because the truth is, I don't know myself. "I haven't got a clue, really," I tell her. "I'll always be honest with you, Sasha. If I knew, I would tell you."

"They're going to do something, and you're going to get dragged into it!" Sasha says, throwing a worried glance over at me.

"Probably," I admit. "And the night was going so well too. I mean, we covered all the Valentine's bases..."

"No, we didn't!" Sasha says. Her tone is so sharp that I lean forward to get a better look at her in the dim lights from the dash-board, and I see the tears threatening to fall from her eyes.

"Sweetheart, no, don't worry about me," I try to soothe her, but she hushes me with a wave of her hand before swiping at her eyes.

"We didn't cover all the bases!" she says. "You got to third, sure, but I didn't even get to second with you! Dammit, Chase, I wanted to hit a home run tonight!"

"You wanted...a home run?" I chuckle before I burst into outright laughter. "Sweetheart, I'll let you walk all my bases anytime you want," I joke with her, trying to make her feel better. We're almost at the clubhouse, and I don't want her leaving me upset.

"You know you're my first, Chase," Sasha whispers. "You mean so much to me, and if anything happened to you, I..."

"Nothing is going to happen to me," I say, interrupting her sentence, but not her thoughts. "I'm going to be fine, and together we'll make your first time magical, I promise you that."

"No, goofball, not my first dick!" Sasha snorts. "I mean, yeah, you're the first one of those too, but you're my first... I love you, Chase Fury. I love you, and if this club takes you away from me, I swear to God, I'll burn their clubhouse down. You hear me?"

Sasha had pulled into the Savage Kings clubhouse parking lot as she said this, stopping the Mustang just behind a group of police cars and an ambulance. She's still looking straight ahead, as though she's afraid to see my reaction.

"Come here, sweetheart," I tell her softly as I cup the side of her face. I turn her towards me, our lips crashing together in a kiss that is so fierce our teeth clash from our awkward position. "I've loved you for weeks now," I tell her as I break away. "It might have been the moment I saw you, hell, I don't know. I just know that you're every-thing to me, and the only reason I didn't stand outside your house singing my love to you was because I thought it was too fast, and I'd scare you away."

"My parents would have tried to chase you away, your singing is awful." Sasha laughs, her hands tangled in the back of my hair. "Go,

Chase. Do whatever you have to do. Text me tonight and let me know you're okay, then I'll see you in the morning. Deal?"

"Deal," I agree. "I love you, Sasha. God, you're going to get sick of hearing it from me, I'm going to be shouting it everywhere I go."

"I love you too, Chase," she says as she pulls me in for one more kiss.

I finally have to pull her hands down from my head so I can get going, but I lean back in for one more quick peck before I jump out of the car. "Get on out of here before these boys decide to ask any questions," I tell her, nodding to the police cars. I close the door, then wave as she backs out of the lot.

I can see more blue lights on the horizon coming from town, and I know our time is short. I've thought it over, and I might have an idea why Reese wanted me here. With April dead, they had to bring in the police immediately. Robbie will undoubtedly tell them everything he knows, and that will lead them straight to Brian Lehmann. Brian will never give any information to the police, that's just basic outlaw code. But if we can get to him first...well, we have ways to make people talk.

I'm walking over to the clubhouse when a low whistle gets my attention. Reese is standing to the side of the building, and once he knows he has my attention, he gestures sharply for me to come to him. I follow him out back, where a black cargo van sits, idling. Reese opens the side door and motions for me to jump into the back seat.

Once I'm inside, I see Fast Eddie is sitting in the driver's seat. "Hey, boy," he greets me as Reese steps up into the van and then quietly closes the passenger side door. "Deacon and Rubin are inside dealing with the police and that boy, Robbie. The three of us are off to make a house call."

"You know where Lehmann is?" I ask Eddie. I'm surprised when it's Reese who answers.

"Knowing he was expelled from your school last year made it easy to get contact information," Reese says. "From there, I got all of the phone numbers on their family wireless plan. Then I tracked all of those phones. The phones assigned to Brian Lehmann and his parents are currently pinging together, at the same address the school files have as his home. Once I accessed their home security cameras, I could see that they are currently on their back porch, cooking what appear to be steaks and potatoes. We should be there before they're done baking," Reese concludes.

I stare, wide-eyed, at the back of his head, in awe not just that he spoke so much at once, but at what he was able to find out in such a short amount of time. After a moment, my mind latches onto the most immediate concern, given that Reese has already covered so much ground. "We know where he is and what he's doing...what are *we* doing? I mean, what's the plan here?"

Fast Eddie glances at me in the rearview mirror. "I'm going to drive you young'uns over there lickety-split, then you two are going to counsel the Lehmann family on the error of their ways, as it were. You get the idea?"

"A girl died," Reese pronounces in a solemn voice. "A price has to be paid."

"What the hell are you talking about?" I demand. "The police are going to be there in no time. Are you planning on murdering the family and just walking off?"

"No," Reese says.

"Settle down, boy," Eddie grunts. "Y'all ain't gonna kill nobody unless they make ya. You're thinking with your head, and not your emotions, boy. That's good, that's real good. We got to make sure these fellas understand that they broke *our* laws, selling drugs 'round here and hurting people. Now, I'm heartbroken about that poor girl dying, that's the Lord's truth, but we need to see if these fellas knew them drugs were deadly, or if it was just a terrible accident. The police will handle most of this, but if this was the Aryan boys passing out this shit, well, they know the rules 'round here. We've made it real clear to them before. They're going to have to suffer our punishment as well, you see?"

"Of course, I get that, I'm just trying to figure out what you guys mean by 'our punishment'? If you want to hand them an ass-whooping, you know I'm all aboard and I'll give it everything I've got. But look, Reese," I say as I lean up and place a hand on his shoulder. "You've got to understand, man, you're hard to read. If you're planning on walking in there and murdering this dude and his family in cold blood, you have to let me know."

"Could you?" Reese asks, looking over his shoulder to watch my reaction.

I don't even hesitate before answering. "No. I could kill a man if he deserved it, or if he was a threat, without a second thought. Hell, maybe this dude who sold the drugs *does* deserve it. But you said there were other people there, some family members. I won't kill someone that wasn't involved, and that's the end of it. If you want to take my cut for it, so be it."

"Good," Reese says, as he turns back around.

Eddie lets out a chuckle as he turns off the highway onto a side road, then says, "Boy sounds just like Deacon sometimes. We're almost there, they've gotta place down in the woods back here. I'm gonna let you out up the road a bit. You can traipse through the trees and get a look at 'em, then make your move."

Reese nods, then turns to look back at me. He takes a deep breath and braces himself, as though preparing for some unpleasant task, before he says, "The Savage Kings are not murderers. We are killers. You already understand the distinction. I will not kill this drug dealer for what he has done. Death is too easy, too quick. Death is mercy. What he has done requires suffering. We will make sure the drugs are removed from our streets and begin administering pain for the insult they have committed us. The pain may be physical, emotional, financial...I will decide once we face them. Are you ready?"

The van comes to a stop, and I give a sharp nod as I open my door. I thought I had gotten to know Reese a bit during our time together the last few weeks. While I was certain he was a hard-ass, it seemed as though he had strict convictions he adhered to. His words tonight confirmed it. I don't know much of anything about his past, but I do know he's loyal, fierce, and honest. I can trust him to do the right thing.

Reese hops down from the van and leads me to the rear doors. He opens them both to reveal a large gun safe, which he quickly opens with a numerical code. He lifts the lid and picks up an assault rifle, slaps a clip into it, then slings it over his shoulder by the strap, the barrel pointing towards the ground. Reaching back in, he pulls out two holstered pistols, handing one to me.

I check the clip while he tucks his into a holster under his arm. I just hold onto mine, since I don't have anything else to carry. Reese pulls a shotgun out of the box and a belt filled with shells, which he quickly loads into the gun. Once the shotgun is loaded, I think he is going to hand it to me, but instead, he slams the doors on the van and nods towards the woods, already moving away.

"You want me to carry anything else?" I whisper as we hit the tree line.

"No," Reese replies. A few seconds later, he adds, "I've never seen you shoot."

"I'm decent," I explain. "Grew up with guns, I know how to handle them."

"You are loud," Reese says in a tone that doesn't invite further conversation.

He takes a slight lead, somehow able to easily pick a trail through the underbrush. Only a minute later, a clearing comes into view ahead of us, the sounds of feminine laughter and rougher voices carrying to us in the evening air.

"How did you get us straight here?" I whisper.

Reese looks at me and gives a pronounced sniff in reply, his nostrils flaring. Then he taps the side of his nose to make sure I get the point. I take a deep breath and realize that I can smell charcoal burning—the grill Reese told me about earlier.

We creep right up to the edge of the tree line in their backyard. From there, we can clearly see an older man and woman on the porch, sitting in lounge chairs and drinking beer. A younger man is standing at the grill, using a pair of tongs to flip foil wrapped potatoes as they bake.

"Just like you said," I whisper.

Reese points towards the deck where they're sitting and whispers, "Tiki torches. The light will blind them to our approach until we step into their radius. Stay out of the light until I whistle. They'll think the darkness holds more of us. We hold them at gunpoint, explain the situation, and then take corrective action."

"Corrective action?" I hiss, but Reese is already striding through the backyard with the shotgun in his hands. In a few quick steps, I fall in behind him, but make sure to hang back as he approaches the flickering circle of light cast into the yard.

"Brian Lehmann!" Reese roars as he steps into the light at the foot of the porch. The explosive change from his normal tone is so jarring it even startles me, so it's no surprise that the woman screams and the man beside her falls out of his chair.

The man by the grill stands frozen in wide-eyed shock as Reese mounts the stairs, racking the shotgun and leveling it at him as he approaches. "Are you Brian Lehmann?" Reese barks, stopping several feet away.

"Y-yeah," Brian stutters, raising his hands in the air while still holding the tongs. The older man lying on the porch begins to scramble to his feet, but Reese quickly turns the shotgun on him.

"Stay down, Mr. Lehmann. Mrs. Lehmann, I presume?" Reese asks the woman, in a more cordial tone. "Please stay seated."

The man on the ground rolls to a seated position, and they all raise their hands over their heads. "You...you're one of those bikers, the Savage Kings," Mr. Lehmann says from his seat on the porch, as he looks over Reese's cut. "What the hell do you want? We haven't caused you any problems!"

"Of course you have," Reese replies, his voice lowering to a growl. "They don't send me for social calls, Mr. Lehmann. I'm not what you would call the 'face of public relations.' Your Aryan brothers sent you a shipment of drugs for distribution. You've been dealing in our area."

"Bullshit!" Mr. Lehmann snorts. "I don't know how you found out about the drugs, but if this is a shakedown, don't fucking lie about it. I know better than to sell in Emerald Isle."

"Does he?" Reese asks, turning the gun back towards Brian, who is visibly trembling.

"Dad, I didn't know," he whispers.

"What?" his father yells as he scrambles to his feet. "What the fuck did you do?"

Reese lets out a sharp whistle, and I immediately jog forward with my pistol leveled on the elder Lehmann.

"Easy now, Mr. Lehmann," Reese hisses. "Moving too quickly might cause some of my brothers' fingers to twitch."

All three of the Lehmanns stare at me in shock, then cast terrified looks at the darkness around the home. "Oh Jesus," Mrs. Lehmann murmurs, before her voice becomes shrill. "I told you to get away from them, told you not to mess with this shit!"

"Shut up!" Reese snaps. "Brian has been selling those pills you acquired at the local schools, haven't you, boy?"

Brian glances at his father, then nods. "I didn't know," he repeats. "Dad, I wanted to help, prove I could earn. I wanted to be a part of..."

"Shut up," Mr. Lehmann growls, before turning to Reese. "Look, the boy fucked up, and I'll pay you whatever you need to make this right. We can work this out..."

"It's too late for that," Reese says. "A high school girl died tonight. Died after taking whatever tainted shit you sold her. The police were called. They know where she got the drugs. They're on their way here to collect you, Brian."

"Oh my god." Mrs. Lehmann gasps, before bursting into tears. "What have you done?" she shrieks.

"That wasn't supposed to happen," Mr. Lehmann whispers. "They told us they were trying to manufacture ecstasy, but that some of the pills weren't right. They never said anything about..."

"As I said, it's too late for excuses," Reese interrupts. "Where's the rest of the shipment?"

"It's in the house," Mr. Lehmann admits, waving towards the sliding glass door behind him.

"Step into the yard," Reese orders the family, motioning with the shotgun. "Remember, my associates are covering you," he adds as they file past him, coming down the stairs to stand in a line a few feet away from me. Mrs. Lehmann is sobbing while wrapping her arms around her son. She whispers something that sounds like 'stupid little shit' to him before she chokes up and becomes incoherent.

Reese places the shotgun over his shoulder, then slides open the door at the back of the house. "Anyone in there?" he turns and asks the family.

"No, no one else," Mr. Lehmann says. "No one will surprise you if you want to check the house."

"Any pets?" Reese asks, surprising everyone.

"Pets? No, no pets..." Mr. Lehmann trails off as he sees Reese pick up a bottle of lighter fluid sitting on the porch railing, which he pops open and then tosses inside on the carpet. "No, oh no," he continues to groan, as Reese walks back over to the charcoal grill.

"Don't worry," Reese says. "The police will be here soon to pick up your son. If the fire has time to consume your drug stash, I may even be doing you a favor." With that, he kicks the grill over into the home, sparks flying as the charcoal clatters across the carpet. I can't see the fire at first, only a stream of smoke drifting around Reese that quickly begins to thicken. A moment later, flames race up the curtain by the sliding glass door and are soon licking all around the doorway.

Reese walks back down the steps and joins me, both of us staring at the Lehmanns for the next few minutes, as the fire spreads throughout this side of the home. Other than Mrs. Lehmann's sobbing, no one makes a sound until Reese finally breaks the silence.

"That will do." He nods. "Remember our laws, Mr. Lehmann, if you intend to do further business with the Aryans. I don't like repeating myself." Slapping me lightly on the arm, Reese backs away into the darkness and then leads me towards the tree line.

We don't speak as we move quickly through the woods, circling back around to the side road where we left Eddie. Reese breaks into a jog once we're clear of the trees, heading straight for the side door of the van. He opens it up and jumps inside, then waves me in and pulls the doors shut, the van already in motion.

Reese begins carefully unloading his guns, placing magazines on the seat between us while shotgun shells go into a cupholder. As Eddie guides the van back up to the main road, he pauses at a stop sign, looking back at us. His gaze drifts out the rear window, where the night sky is beginning to glow from what appears to be a fire in the near distance.

"Decide on a bit of arson tonight?" Eddie asks.

"It was convenient," Reese agrees. "The boy, Brian, was only about the age of the Prospect. He's young and stupid. When he realized what he had done, he was broken. The fire is a reminder to the father. The police, the courts...they can handle the rest."

"Aren't they going to tell the cops we were there? That we did this?" I ask Reese.

"Probably not." Reese shrugs. "If Mr. Lehmann does, he's admitting that his home was burned due to the drugs he was keeping. The police will find evidence of them, almost certainly. That will cause him much more problems than an 'accident with the grill.'"

"There are lots of other reasons he'll keep his mouth shut," Eddie interjects. "You don't worry about that none, boy. Did he do all right out there?" he asks Reese, jerking his head at me.

"Fine," Reese grunts. "Get us back to the clubhouse. Our alibi is that we never left. We were in the back the entire time."

I hand the pistol Reese gave me back to him once he's done with the other weapons. Remembering that I need to text Sasha, I pull out my phone and send her a quick note.

"Hey sweetheart, just wanted to say good night. I'm going to crash

*at the clubhouse tonight. I'll have one of the guys drop me off at school
in the morning. See you then. I love you."*

I hit send on that message, then send another one to my parents,
telling them roughly the same thing. After that, I stare out the
window in silence, trying to fight the gnawing anxiety in my belly.
The night has been exhilarating, horrifying, and exhausting. Sasha
and I proclaimed our love, a friend of mine killed a girl, and I helped
burn down some skinhead drug dealer's home.

Eddie kills the lights on the van as we creep up a backroad to
come in behind our clubhouse. Once he parks, we all pile out, quietly
shutting the doors and going in through the back entrance. Eddie and
Reese both go immediately to the massive industrial refrigerator in
the kitchen area and pull out bottles of beer, which they crack open
and then tap together before drinking. I walk past them and head on
into the main room to see if Robbie is still there.

The main room has been cleared, and from the way the lights are
turned down, I assume that Deacon has closed up the clubhouse to
any non-members for the evening. He and Rubin are sitting at the
bar, a bottle of whiskey between them.

"How'd it go, kid?" Rubin Brady, the club's VP and founding
member, asks as I pull up a stool beside Deacon.

"Anyone else here?" I ask before I answer his question.

"Nah, I wouldn't ask if there were," Rubin replies.

"Nothing to it." I shrug. "We found them on their back porch,
having a cookout. Reese talked to them about what had happened.
The father didn't know the kid had been dealing locally. He was
pissed. When we told them the drugs killed a local, the kid broke
down and his momma held him while she chewed him out."

"You kill anybody?" Rubin asks.

"Nah. Reese set their house on fire and we left."

Deacon downs a shot in front of him then pours another one out
of the bottle on the counter. "Good," he says. "Police arrested your
friend, that kid, Robbie. He was already telling them everything
before they even asked. Poor kid ain't got a hair on his sack, does he?"

I snort, but then shake my head sadly. "He was just looking for a good time. He asked me to get him some weed, but I told him no way."

"He didn't mention that part. That's good, that he kept your name out of his mouth," Rubin says.

"Yeah, yeah it is. I'm going to miss that dumb son-of-a-bitch, though."

"You'll see him soon enough," Deacon says. "He was partly responsible, but if he helps them nail down the dealer, they'll go easy on him. Here, Chase." Deacon slides the shot glass over to me. "Knock that back and go get some sleep. You got school tomorrow, don't you?"

I nod, then pick up the shot glass and toss it back with a grimace. It stings my nose and burns my throat, but I'll be damned if it doesn't also ease the knot I had in my stomach. "Thanks, Deacon," I say, as I slide the glass back to him. "I'm going to go find my pillow and warm it up for a few hours. I'll see you boys in the morning."

"I'll be up here about half past seven, and take you to school," Deacon says. "Your woman dropped you off here, right?"

I nod, then grin like an idiot at the thought of 'my woman.' As I head downstairs to my room, I pull my phone out and see that Sasha has replied to me.

"*Goodnight, Chase. I love you. You loaded my bases tonight, and I expect you to clean them up soon.*"

I manage to fall asleep easily with that beautiful thought in mind, visions of Sasha sweeping away the ugliness of everything else that had transpired.

CHAPTER ELEVEN

When Deacon drops me off outside my shop class the next morning, I'm surprised to find that Sasha's Mustang isn't parked right up by the building in its spot of honor. I'm a little later than normal today, but since Mr. Aikens is still sitting out on the step, smoking his pipe, I don't think too much of it. I'm sure she's just running a little behind after the night we had.

I sit down beside Mr. Aikens and pull out a fresh pack of cigarettes I snagged at the clubhouse. Lighting one up, I lean back on the stairs and look over to my teacher, who is eyeing me suspiciously.

"Morning, Mr. Aikens. How you holding up today?" I ask him.

"Other than my bowels feeling like they're welded shut? I'm fine." He puffs at me, the sweet-smelling smoke enveloping both of us. "I was wondering if anyone was going to show up today. Your friend Robbie isn't here, a couple of other guys are out. Oh, and your girlfriend showed up looking as though you two were still on a date."

"What?" I say, taken aback. "Sasha is already here? Where's the car?"

"Beats me." Mr. Aikens shrugged. "She came up the sidewalk in heels and this little white flowery dress. Look, Chase, I need you to talk to her. We're going to be doing some work with the grinders today, and I can't have her in the shop with so much, uh...so much skin exposed."

I stare at him in shock, not really knowing how to respond. Finally, I take a drag off my cigarette before grinding it out on the step. "I'll talk to her," I say, then throw the butt away before adding, "I think Robbie might be out for a bit. I'll let you know what I hear."

I stomp inside the building with my heart racing, unable to anticipate what surprise Sasha may have pulled out for me today. When I see her over by the drafting board, I stop short in my tracks. She is bent slightly forward, and the loosely flowing floral dress she's wearing is short enough to draw the eye of even the most stoic of monks. One of my classmates is over by the tools on the far wall, but his head is about to twist off his neck as he strains to see if the dress rises any further.

"Hey!" I yell at him, practically snarling as his gaze snaps to me. He ducks his head and blushes furiously before turning back to the wrenches he was pretending to examine.

Sasha turns at my call too, and breaks into a huge smile when she sees me. Her heels practically spark on the concrete floor as she saunters over to me, the sway of her breasts and the outline of her nipples through the thin fabric clearly indicating she is going braless again today.

I don't realize I'm slack-jawed until she's face to face with me and leans in for a kiss, grinning impishly the entire time. She presses herself into me in a hug that is positively indecent, rubbing the entire front of her body against me as my cock strains mightily to rip out the thigh of my pants.

"Well, you're happy to see me, aren't you?" she whispers into my ear. "I think I overheard Mr. Aikens say I couldn't do any grinding today. Are you going to listen to him? Or are you going to let me"—she rubs herself against me again before finishing —"grind?"

"Where?" I whisper hoarsely as I wrap my arms around her, squeezing her so tightly her breasts flatten against me. "When?"

"I'll show you the answers to those," she says. "But if you ask me *how*, Chase Fury, I'm going to be disappointed in you."

"All right, break it up, you two," Mr. Aikens says, as he pulls the door closed behind him. "Come on, let's go take roll and get this test knocked out. Chase, did you get a chance to, er..."

"Ah, yes, we discussed that very thing," I tell him, while still staring into Sasha's eyes.

"Good, good. Well, you two just hang back while we're doing lab later on, after we finish up the classwork. Come along now."

Mr. Aikens walks past us without another glance. Sasha grabs my hand, and together we head over to the classroom, where everyone else is already seated. The test doesn't take us long to complete, and once we've all handed in our papers, Mr. Aikens leads the class back out to the shop floor.

"Come on," Sasha says, pulling my arm to hang back as the rest of the class follows the teacher. Once we're behind the rest of the group, she leads me out the rear door and down the back steps.

"Where are we heading, sweetheart?" I grin at her. "You don't seem to have a car."

"I parked it at the very end of the lot, away from everyone else. No one ever parks out there, it's too far to walk. We should have all the privacy we need." Sasha winks at me.

She doesn't need to tell me anything else. We still have the entirety of third period before we would even be missed, and my cock is so swollen, I can barely run to keep up with her as she leads me through the lot. Sasha pulls her keys out of the small purse she retrieved from the classroom, and a moment later, we're crammed into the front seats of her Mustang.

I've already shrugged out of my cut and tossed it into the back seat, my t-shirt quickly following. Sasha practically lunges at me, our lips crashing together and tongues mingling as her hands fumble with my belt buckle. I reach down to help her get the clasp undone, but then she takes over, jerking my jeans and boxers all the way down to my knees.

"Oh shit, Chase," she murmurs as my cock leaps free and slaps against my belly. I can't tell if the look on her face is shock or dismay as she watches my cock throb inches from her face, and after a moment, I burst out laughing.

"Are you okay?" I manage to gasp, as her eyes rove over my body before coming back up to my face.

She moves over, straddling me to kiss me again, my hands roaming under the hem of her dress and squeezing handfuls of her gorgeous, round ass. "I can't believe how good I feel, Chase," she whispers. "But ask me again later. From the looks of things, I might be a bit sore."

My hands slide from her ass up to her hips, dragging her dress up her body as her lips move down my chest. She nips at my pecs and licks my abs as I continue to tug at her dress, then she rubs a hand down the length of my shaft before leaning back and raising her arms. I lift her dress up to her tits, then she grabs the hem and drags it over her head, tossing it into the growing pile in the back seat. As she leans back from me, I take in every inch of her glorious body, noticing that the thin landing strip of pubic hair she has left unshaven is already exposed.

"Panties in the glovebox again?" I tease her.

"You know it." She grins as she leans down to press her entire body against me, the feeling of her nude flesh against mine is so overwhelming my cock bucks against her belly. "Easy there, soldier, I'll get to you in a moment," she whispers as she begins to lick her way back down my body. She drags her tongue across the ridges of my stomach and she lowers herself to the floorboard, then her left hand reaches down to cup my balls, while her right one wraps around my cock and guides the tip to her lips.

"Oh Christ, Sasha," I groan as she strokes my shaft, her tongue wrapping around the head of my cock and licking frantic circles before she tries to slide more of it into her mouth. An involuntary spasm racks me as her teeth briefly rake the underside of my cock, and she backs off to look at me in horror.

"Oh shit, I'm sorry, Chase. It's so big, I..." she stammers.

I grin at her, overwhelmed by her beauty and her frantic expression, as though she broke my cock. "We learn by doing," I tell her, quoting Mr. Aikens.

"And we do it until we get it right," she finishes, beaming back at me. Her left hand never stopped caressing my balls, and once she's reassured, she leans down and licks my cock instead, starting at the base and letting her tongue linger on every inch until she reaches the tip. She tries once again to fit it into her mouth, taking slow bobbing strokes until half my shaft disappears.

Releasing my balls, Sasha continues holding onto my length, rubbing it as she holds as much of it as she can into her mouth. I see her free hand reach down between her legs and feel the motion of her tongue become more frantic and erratic as she begins rubbing herself while sucking me. She starts moaning around me, the sound and vibration so intense, my abdomen tenses as I fight the urge to climax with every ounce of my will.

"Fuck, Sasha, that's incredible!" I cry, so loud that she gasps, her head popping up as my chest heaves and my cock bulges in her hand. I grab her upper arms and drag her up, our lips meeting again, our hands and mouths frantic for every inch of flesh they can find.

I grab her ass again in both hands, jerking her to me and forcing a moan from her lips as the head of my cock presses briefly against her pussy.

"Please, Chase, please, I'm ready," Sasha moans. "I want this, I need you so badly..."

"Do you have a condom?" I ask her, as my hands come around and find her breasts, forcing them together as I wrap my lips around each of her stiff nipples.

"We don't need one, I have terrible periods," she says as she grabs my face and bucks her hips, her lower body desperately seeking my cock.

I pause for a moment, uncertain if I should risk spoiling the mood by questioning her understanding of pregnancy. After a moment, I decide to go with my best, confused, "What?"

"I have terrible periods," she repeats as she forces my head back down to her tit. "I take the pill for them."

"Ah!" I tell her nipple as I lick my way around it. "Say no more, sweetheart. I won't be able to, for a bit." My hand roams lower, finding the trail of her pubic hair and following it down until I feel her clit.

As the pad of my thumb continues teasing her swollen button, I press my middle finger against her damp entrance and gently press it inside of her.

"Holy shit!" Sasha cries, and I have to grab her hip with my free hand to keep her from bucking away.

"More?" I ask to make sure.

"Yes. Just like that, Chase. Yes, yes, oh god..." she chants before her moans become incoherent.

Her hips bounce, and her hands dig into my hair as she slams her pussy down on my fingers. Seconds later, her back arches and spasms rack her body. Once they finally subside, Sasha collapses against my chest.

Grabbing her chin, I bring her mouth to mine so that our tongues can meet again, one of my arms wrapping around her to cradle her neck, the other reaching under her thigh to cup her ass and pull her to me.

"Are you ready?" I ask her, the head of my cock already pressing against her slick entrance, pulsing steadily, as though knocking for entry.

"You're mine, Chase Fury," she growls as she pulls my lips back down to hers, rolling her hips and pushing against me so that the head of my cock presses deeper inside. She moans into my mouth as I tighten my grip on her, then slowly, she lowers her body a little at a time until I feel her body tense up in my arms.

"Take your time, sweetheart," I say. I know she's a virgin, and I have no idea how painful this must be for her. "If it's too much too soon, just say so."

"I'll tell you when it's too much," she replies, locking eyes with me. "I want to love you slow and easy today. But after this first time... I want you to fuck me. You fuck me as hard and long as you can, you...*OH!*" She moans and trembles as her clit rubs the base of my cock. She had rolled her hips on that last stroke, completely impaling herself as she sank down on me.

"That's it, baby," I tell her as my cock stretches her to accommodate every inch, setting up shop in his brand-new home.

"You're inside me," she whispers, blue eyes wide in awe as our gaze locks.

"Never gonna leave either, sweetheart," I assure her.

Our mouths meet again, the only other words that pass between us the next few moments are professions of our love for each other. Soon, her hands drop from cradling my head to holding on to my shoulders, then Sasha spreads her thighs a little further so that she can take even more of me. My hands roam all the way down to her gorgeous ass as she rides me. On each thrust, she grinds down a little longer, a little harder.

"Oh god, Chase, I'm so full and so close," she moans as she arches against me, her breasts trembling as her pussy clamps down on my cock. All I can do is hold her tighter to me, closer, and clench my teeth to hold myself off as she comes apart with sharp gasps of pleasure.

Once she relaxes against my chest again, she meets my gaze with her eyes half-lidded, looking for all the world as though she's drunk.

"You didn't...yet?" she asks as she squirms on my still-swollen cock.

"No, but if you're too sore, we can stop," I tell her, even though it may damn well kill me to pull out of her right now.

Without another word, Sasha rolls her hips again, rubbing her clit against the base of my cock. "Fuck me, Chase," she whispers.

"You sure about that?" I ask, and she nods.

Unable to wait another second, I reach for the seat lever to lower us, then I roll her over with our bodies still connected so that I'm on top of her.

On my first, deep, heavenly thrust, I bury myself inside of her and Sasha cries out.

"Yes!" she says before I can worry about whether or not she can take it. "Fuck me," she urges, so I do.

I'm almost certain our cries of pleasure can be heard from inside the school half a mile away as we ravage each other, our lovemaking turning into something so fierce and primal the Mustang shakes and trembles as though the engine is running. There's nothing gentle in the way Sasha digs her nails into me, clawing and scratching at my ass as she strains to slam my cock into her harder and harder.

When I feel my balls begin to tighten and the pressure building at the base of my cock, I increase my pace even further, determined to bring her over the edge with me. "Fuck, Sasha, I love you so damn much," I pant, crushing her to me in a bruising hug as I hammer away at her.

Instead of replying verbally, she throws her head back violently, her tits completely flattened against my chest. The walls of her pussy squeeze down on my cock but are unable to stop my relentless hammering as my orgasm explodes deep inside of her. Our break-neck pace continues for a few more seconds before we both collapse in a sweaty heap, our bodies damp from our frantic fucking.

I get an elbow under me so I can keep most of my weight off of Sasha, but I pull her leg over mine and keep my cock buried inside of her as we recover. "What do you think about making this our new lunchtime routine?" I ask her.

Her hand is thrown over her head, her hair spread all around behind her. She reaches up to touch my face as she laughs, still gently rolling her hips to press into me. "I think we'll need to bring towels," she replies. "I had no idea it would be this...wet!"

"It's only sloppy when it's good." I grin.

"Then we're very sloppy, because it was very, very good," she says as she pulls me back down for another kiss. We stay entangled together in the passenger seat until the sound of a distant bell ringing brings both our heads up, straining to hear.

"Is that the lunch bell?" Sasha asks.

"Yeah, must be time." I sigh. I begin to pull away from Sasha, both of us breaking into laughter as our skin practically peels apart.

"Oh God, everyone is going to be able to tell we've been fucking, aren't they?" Sasha asks.

"Well, if we go back inside like this, yeah," I assure her, pointing at my cock that I finally pulled free from her. "Once you get your dress back on and I tuck this away, hopefully people will just think we just tried really hard in gym today."

"You don't even have P.E.!" Sasha protests.

"Yeah, but everyone thinks I'm dirty anyhow. It's the leather," I reply. "Don't worry, sweetheart, freshly fucked looks amazing on you. God, I love you, Sasha." My cock begins to pulse at this proclamation, slowly swelling as though eager to express its own sentiments.

Sasha looks me up and down, biting her lip and leaning towards me, as though she's ready to meet the challenge. With a sigh, though, she reaches into the back seat and grabs her dress. "I love you too, Chase Fury. Let's get done with this school day, and I'll text my parents to let them know we're going out this afternoon. Do you know anywhere private we can go, so we can continue this...discussion?" she asks, giving my half-erect cock a meaningful look.

"Oh sweetheart, I'm gonna take you, and I mean 'take you' all over this world. Come on, baby, let's go knock out these classes. Then, you and me, well...we've got nothing but good times ahead of us."

CHAPTER TWELVE

"You all right over there, man? You go to sleep on me?" Abe asks from where he's sitting cross-legged on his bunk.

"Nah, man, I'm awake," I reply, letting go of the old memories and drifting back down to the shitty cell block.

"You got quiet for a while, after telling me about how that boy Reese handled those skinheads and burned that place down. It sounds like your brothers are a rowdy bunch. I like them already. What happened next?"

What happened next was that I made love to the woman I wanted to spend the rest of my life with. The woman I still think about every day. The woman who broke me.

I've tried to suppress the thoughts of Sasha and just give Abe the highlights of my time with the Savage Kings over the last few weeks that we've been getting to know each other. There really isn't much else to do to pass the time. It's been harder than I could have imagined, trying to give him an idea of what prospecting is like while trying to separate all the time she and I spent together.

123

"What happened next was more of the same, really," I tell Abe. "After that kid Brian got arrested and no heat came down on the club, my brothers took me down to the tattoo parlor and I got my first ink, my first MC symbols on my bicep. I liked it so much, I went back and got my sleeve done just a week later. I kept training with Reese and doing grunt work for the club. After they were sure I could drive the tow truck anytime they needed, they taught me bartending, even though I was underage. Once Reese was satisfied I could hold my own in a fight, they even had me doing some security work. Once my year was up, I officially patched in, and the rest is history."

"Those guys have stood by you through everything, and are watching your back, even now," Abe observes. "If they would be willing, I'd like to talk to them."

"That's good." I flash Abe a grin. "Because when I made a call to the clubhouse a few weeks ago to tell them about my deal with T.J., they said they want to come out and meet you next visitation. They're already making the arrangements."

"Damn, Chase, I don't know what to say except, I guess, thank you. I mean it, you helping me out here and offering me all this...I'll do anything I can to make it good. I mean it," Abe says.

"You sound like you're getting a little choked up over there, big guy," I chide him gently. "Don't think so hard about it, man. You might not believe it, but I can tell you're worth it. You're going to be one hell of a brother in the MC. It's been good to meet you in here and have someone to talk to. Now, though, I'm gonna try to get some sleep tonight."

"Yeah, I hear you. Good night, man," Abe says.

"Good night to you too, Abe."

As I roll over, my thoughts turn back to my time prospecting, and all the details I couldn't bring myself to talk about out loud—buying my Fat Boy with Sasha, our adventures in her Mustang, the conversations, the sex...hell, *all* my time with her. I have to pay close attention and stop myself every night before her name leaves my lips. Most of my days prospecting with the club was just more of the same routine, while my time with Sasha...well, it overwhelms everything in my memories. Especially my memories of *that* night, our last night together...

CHAPTER THIRTEEN

2008

"I fucking love seeing my name on your skin," I tell Sasha. Bringing her wrist up to my lips, I place a kiss just below the small, black cursive letters. While her new tattoo is only a few inches wide, it may as well be the size of a fucking Mack truck for how damn hard my cock is right now, knowing she's mine.

"Good, because it's sort of permanent," Sasha replies with a grin. Her big, blue eyes sparkling up at me from underneath the street-lamps are full of adoration and love I don't deserve. And God, she's so fucking beautiful it hurts. I was a goner from the second I saw her.

"Permanent is exactly why I like it," I tell her as I wrap my arms around her lean waist to drag her body against mine.

Sasha pushes open the leather cut that I'm wearing, with no shirt underneath, to run her fingernail carefully around my fresh ink — her name that's written in thick, black cursive letters on the left side of my chest.

"My parents are gonna be so pissed when they find out," she says. Her smile grows even wider, which is no surprise. I quickly learned my girl gets off on excitement and danger, anything her parents would threaten to whoop her ass over, even though she just turned eighteen.

"So what if they are?" I ask. "They're always pissed at you lately, ever since you started seeing me."

"Very true, it's just..."

When she lowers her eyes and pauses, I grab her chin between my thumb and finger to make her look at me. "Just what?"

"What if it's bad luck?" she asks as her front teeth nervously work over her bottom lip.

"What's bad luck?"

"Doesn't everyone say it's the kiss of death for all relationships if you get your lover's name tattooed on you? I mean, what if my parents are right and we *are* moving too fast, Chase?"

"Shh, calm down baby." I grasp her gorgeous, flawless face between both of my palms. "Fast is the only fucking way that I know how to move. And it's *not* bad luck or anything else," I assure her. "That's just a bunch of superstitious bullshit. Because you and me? We're fucking forever, sweetheart. I'm so damn certain of that, I would make you my old lady right now, if I could. I have *zero* fucking doubts that you're the only woman I'll ever want."

"Seriously?" she asks as her eyes start to glisten under the glow of the lights in the parking lot. "You would marry me and give up all the clubhouse sluts?"

"Hell yes," I say without any hesitation. Before Sasha and I got together, I slept with a handful of the girls that hang around the *Savage Asylum*, the bar that also houses the Savage Kings MC's clubhouse. Those women will fuck anything in leather, even prospects like me, still trying to patch in. I haven't touched a single one of them since Sasha and I started seeing each other six months ago. There isn't a girl in that clubhouse that can turn my head. I'm so certain of what we have that I tell Sasha, "Let's do it. Let's get married tonight. We could fly to Vegas..."

"My parents would never—" she starts to say, but my lips crashing down on hers puts a stop to her words.

When I pull back, I look her in the eyes to let her know I'm dead serious. "Fuck what your parents think. Marry me, and then we'll get our own place and they won't be able to say shit about what we do."

Sasha studies my face for several long seconds, judging my sincerity while I hold my breath. Finally, she says, "Okay."

"Okay?" I repeat with a grin of relief.

"Yes. Oh my god, yes! Why are we still standing here?" she asks excitedly before she slips out of my arms. Sasha strides over to my bike in her sexy strappy heels and white dress. It's way too short for riding on the back of a Harley, which is exactly why I fucking love it. She throws one of her mile-long legs over the seat and then leans forward to grip the handlebars, pushing her amazing ass out and causing her full, perfect tits to nearly spill out of the top of the material.

"Hop on the back. I'll drive us to the airport," Sasha jokes.

"Goddamn, you are so fucking sexy sitting on my Fat Boy," I tell her. Unable to resist getting a photo of her looking like the pin-up girl from every man's wet dream, I pull out my cell phone from my pocket and snap a picture.

After I put my phone away, I go over and climb on behind her. Smoothing my hands up both of her sides, I whisper to her, "*This* is where you fucking belong. Your fine ass was made to sit on my bike." I bury my nose in her long, blonde hair that's lightly blowing in the coastal winds, unable to get enough of her sweet apple scent before my lips go to her neck right below her ear. It's the one spot on her body that I know from months of experience will make her go limp and instantly wet. Sure enough, Sasha shivers and then leans back against my chest, putty in my hands. Fuck, I don't think I'll ever get enough of her. My cock is so hard that riding will be damn near impossible.

"I want you so much, right here, right now. I can't wait a second longer," I whisper in her ear, fucking desperate for her. "If I lift your dress and lower you down onto my cock, you could ride it just like this, and no one would be able to see me buried deep inside of you."

"*Chase*," Sasha moans my name, making my dick swell even more against the fly of my jeans. "Someone could see us."

"Let them watch. I don't give a fuck, because *this* is all mine," I tell Sasha as I ease my hand underneath the front hem of her dress and cup her pussy through her lacy thong.

I know my girl better than anyone, and the thought of someone catching us is turning her on even more. She's been a good girl for the last seventeen years, so she still likes to pretend she's good when, deep down, she's really fucking naughty.

And despite what her parents think, I wasn't a bad influence on her.

"Chase, please," Sasha begs when she squirms against my hand that hasn't moved the way she wants yet. As she rocks her hips, her ass bumps right against the bulge in the front of my jeans that's pressing into her bottom and making me fucking crazy.

"You're gonna come on my fingers, and then I'm gonna fuck you right here," I warn her as I slip my fingers underneath the seam of her panties and penetrate her with just the tip of one.

"*Ohhh God*," she moans as she throws her head back on my shoulder, then covers my hand with her own to force me to go deeper inside of her.

My lips come down on her neck again as my fingers start pumping in and out of her already dripping wet pussy. Her walls clamp down on them, and then her entire body shudders as her orgasm slams into her that damn fast for me.

I don't even give her a chance to recover before I remove my hand from her panties and start undoing my jeans as quick as my shaking hands can go, unable to wait another second to be inside of her.

"Hold those handlebars for me, sweetheart," I tell Sasha, who is still panting when she follows my order. Grasping her hip to hold it steady, I fist my cock with the other hand to line up and slam inside of her pussy so hard, she cries out.

"*Oh, God, Chase!*" she moans. Looking at me over her shoulder, Sasha says, "You feel so good."

"Fuck, yes, baby. Ride me just like that," I tell her. She's hot, tight, and wet. So goddamn perfect that I know I won't last long.

My hands grip both of her hips through her dress, tight enough to leave bruises as I slam her down on my cock, over and over again.

Reaching up, I gather her hair in a ponytail and give it a harsh tug to turn her face to the side so I can kiss her. "I love you...so fucking much," I tell her against her lips.

"I love you too...*ohhh!*" she shouts as she comes again, clenching tightly around my cock, forcing me to follow.

As we both catch our breath and come back down from the clouds together, I kiss her neck and down to her shoulder.

Having Sasha in my arms tonight is so goddamn perfect. Knowing she's agreed to be mine forever makes me fucking euphoric, except...for whatever reason, that happiness is accompanied by something else. My guts are knotting up with fear or...or panic. I've never loved anyone this much before, and it's fucking terrifying worrying about screwing everything up with her.

Are we rushing things? I know I'm ready to marry Sasha, but we're both still young. What if I'm pushing her into something that she'll later regret? We both still have a year of high school left, and then she wants to go to college and study journalism. I'd never try to hold her back on purpose, but what if, by marrying her, she gives up on her dreams to be with me instead?

"Are you sure you want to be my old lady?" I ask her into the silence. "You know I won't ever walk away from the MC, and you want to go to college..."

"I want you more," she says, as she reaches behind her to run her fingers through my hair. "And who said I couldn't have you *and* a degree?"

Still unconvinced, I tell her, "It may not always be easy for us. I'll probably piss you off. There's a reason everyone thinks I'm an asshole."

"We'll have good times and bad," she agrees. "But I love every part of you, even the MC and asshole pieces. They're what make you who you are, Chase."

This.

This is why I fucking love this woman so goddamn much. I don't know why the hell I'm even second-guessing her. She's all-in, right there with me. And unlike some old ladies, she would never ask me to walk away from the club. She knows how important wearing the Savage Kings patch one day soon is to me.

Bringing her face to mine, I kiss the shit out of her until we both have to pull away for oxygen.

"Okay," I say, pushing aside all of those ridiculous doubts or worries, whatever the hell they are. Nothing will change how I feel about Sasha. Ever.

"To the airport?" Sasha asks me when I climb off the back of my bike.

Reaching for her helmet from the handlebar, I kiss the top of her golden head before I put it on her. "Fuck yes," I agree, while fastening her chin strap.

Once her helmet is good and secure, I grab mine and get it in place while Sasha scoots backward to her seat, and I take my place in the front.

"You ready, sweetheart?" I ask, cranking the engine.

"Always," Sasha says. Her words and her arms tightening around my waist so close that the front of her body is flush against my back lets me know she's ready to ride with me—not just today, but every fucking day for the rest of our lives. She trusts me to take care of her and keep her safe.

I may have been a bastard before we met, but she makes me softer because I want to be good to her, good *for* her.

But deep down, I've always known that what her parents say

about me is true—she deserves better than me, and one of these days, I'm probably gonna hurt her beyond repair.

We've stopped for a moment at an intersection, so I reach back to pat her leg reassuringly. Just touching her helps clear the morbid thoughts from my mind.

As the light turns green and the car in front of us clears the intersection, I drop my Fat Boy into gear and ease the throttle, smiling as Sasha reflexively tightens her grip.

The sudden screeching of tires drowns out the roar of my engine. I catch a brief glance of headlights to my right, just before I'm launched into the air.

The next few seconds seem to stretch out endlessly as my body is hurled across the highway. I spin helplessly, briefly blinded by the headlamp on my Harley as my bike's shattered frame twists and sparks across the pavement beneath me. Before I can scream out for Sasha, gravity snatches me back, slamming me into the weedy ditch at the side of the road.

...

A piercing light shines directly into my eyes. When the light disappears, I'm finally able to make out the face, one of a man I've never seen before, hovering over me just inches away in the darkness.

"Who...who the fuck ...wh-what the hell...happened?" I gasp. I try to force myself to sit up, but fall back as a nauseating wave of vertigo washes over me.

"You had a wreck," the stranger's voice tells me slowly. "Try not to move. We're gonna get you to the hospital."

Wreck? Hospital?

My eyes squint as I try to put the world back into focus to figure out what the fuck's happening. The last thing I remember is sitting in the tattoo chair with Sasha beside me, then we were outside the shop on my bike...

Oh, fuck!

"*Sasha?*" I shout in a panic as I struggle to try and sit up again. The asshole with the light pushes my shoulders back down. To hell with him. I shove him out of the way as I sit up again and see the colorful lights of ambulances, firetrucks, and police cars surrounding us.

Then I spot her; Sasha's body is strapped down on a gurney that's being rushed towards an ambulance.

"*SASHA!*" I scream louder and wait for her to answer me, to tell me that she's okay, but she doesn't make a sound.

CHAPTER FOURTEEN

2012

I startle awake, covered in sweat, my hand throbbing from the punch I slammed into the concrete wall of my jail cell. *"She's gone!"* is my first panicked thought, before the full realization and recollection of where I am returns to me.

"You all right over there?" Abe whispers in the darkness. "You were yelling again in your sleep."

"Sorry," I grunt. "I have nightmares. This place will do that to you after a while." Technically, I'm sure that's true, although I've never had any regrets or misgivings about my time in prison. Beating that filthy fucking bastard half to death was a necessity, and I'll serve my time gladly knowing he paid his pound of flesh.

I can't get back to sleep, partly because of the nightmare but mostly because I spend a lot of time every day napping. There isn't much else to do in this place, and every time I try to read one of the tattered books they have available, I invariably start to doze. I'll probably be accused of being all manner of things over the course of my life, but a scholar won't be on the list.

Once our morning roll call is over, the day settles into the same old familiar pattern. Abe has been restless lately. He wanders around the common room occasionally, but invariably ends up stomping back into our cell and collapsing back on his bunk. I don't blame him, I did that a lot too, the first few weeks after I arrived, constantly searching for something new or anything to do to pass the time.

I think it's getting close to our dinner time when a guard enters our cell. I get to my feet, expecting it to be an inspection or something equally mundane. "You both have visitors," the guard announces. "Follow me."

Abe looks at me questioningly. "I've been telling my brothers about you and they wanted to come say hello," I say, waving for him to walk ahead of me. "Let's go see who's here."

Once we're cleared and allowed to enter the visitation room, I immediately spot Deacon and Rubin sitting at a table off in the far corner of the room. I slap Abe on the arm and take the lead, weaving through the jumble of tables where other inmates are visiting with their families. Guards posted around the room keep a wary eye on us, particularly Abe, as we pass.

As I get closer to their table, my smile falters a bit when I notice something off about Deacon. I can't quite place it at first, but as we get to the table, I'm able to make out the thin line of tubing running from his nostrils to a small pack I hadn't been able to see on his back. The old man is wearing a fucking oxygen tank. He hasn't been to visit in a while and I thought he was just busy. Now, I'm starting to think something else has been going on with him that he hasn't told me about over the phone...

Deacon and Rubin both get up, coming around to wrap me up in a hug before stepping back and turning to Abe. "This the one you've been telling me about?" Deacon says, wheezing a little bit before he sits back down.

"This is him," I confirm. "Abraham Cross, this is Deacon Fury, President of the Savage Kings MC, and Rubin Brady, his Vice President. Hell of a royal welcome, all around."

"It's good to meet you two," Abe says as he shakes both of their hands.

We all sit down at the table, but before we can get down to any sort of business, I have to find out what happened to Deacon. "What's going on with that?" I ask my uncle, pointing at his face.

"Hell boy, you ain't been gone that long." Rubin laughs. "He ain't no uglier than he was when you got here."

"You know what I'm talking about," I press him. "Don't try to hide shit from me while I'm here, that isn't how we operate."

"He's right, Rubin." Deacon sighs. "I'll give it to you straight, brother. I've smoked since I was old enough to remember. You combine that with all the other questionable decisions I've made, and it adds up to cancer every time."

"Cancer? Shit!" I exclaim in shock. "You got the oxygen tank, so you must have seen a doctor. How bad is it?" I ask him, dreading the answer.

Deacon glances down at the table for a moment, then says, "It's bad. Started in my lungs, but now...ain't no surgery for this, Chase. I'm scheduled to start some chemotherapy to try and slow it down, but..." He trails off, then directs his attention to Abe. "Fact is," Deacon continues, "every one of us that lives has to pay the same bill eventually. It ain't worth crying over, and it ain't worth dwelling on. You can pour one out for me if you want, when I'm gone. For now, though, I want to talk to this fellow and ask him what manner of silly shit you filled his head with to make him want to sign on with us."

Abe cracks a grin, then leans over the table. He tells them all about what happened the first day he got here, and then goes into his background, recounting the things he's told me about his youth.

"That's it," Abe concludes after only a few minutes. "Same story I'm sure you guys have heard a dozen times from fellows who are interested in finding a family. After the way this one has treated me"—Abe raises one of his huge craggy hands to slap me on the shoulder—"I couldn't help but feel like you all might be just the thing I've hoped to find for me and my little brother."

"So, you're going to get released just a few weeks after Chase?" Rubin asks.

"Yes, sir. Long as I keep my nose clean for the most part, I should be a free man," Abe confirms.

"We normally want a man to prospect for a full year, so we can get the measure of him," Deacon says. "But this is a special circumstance, and I think we can work something out. Abe, I tell you what. You keep watching over our boy Chase all the time he's in here. If you have his back in a place like this, then every man in our MC will know damn well that you'll have theirs too."

"If you can put up with being his cellmate all that time without killing him, we'll know just how serious you are about joining," Rubin interjects with a chuckle.

Deacon waves a hand to silence him as the rest of us share a laugh. "I was going to say that if you can do that, then once you get out of this place, we'll be here to greet you, and hang a prospect cut on you. You'll still need to go through some training, mind you, and everyone will need a chance to get to know you. Even so, with Chase sponsoring you while you two are here, I expect it won't take any time at all to get you voted in as a member. Then, after that, we can talk about letting your brother Gabriel prospect. What do you say, sound like something you want to do?"

"It does, sir," Abe says, his voice cracking. "It feels like a dream, actually. I thought coming in here was going to be the end of me, but to meet Chase, and now his brothers...it's more than I could have ever imagined. Chase is going to get sick of hearing me say it, but thank you. Thank you all for this opportunity."

"Aw hell, boy, don't think of it like that. It's going to be some work," Rubin tells him with a grin. "All families are. But Chase is right, you seem like a good one. Pearls amongst the swine and all that, right?"

"That ain't what that saying means, Rubin, and you damn well know it," Deacon wheezes in irritation. "If you're going to quote the Bible, at least read the thing!"

That sets Abe off into a cackling fit, and I can't help but crack a grin at seeing these two old friends banter. I've missed them, feeling a deep homesickness that only grows more poignant every time they come to visit.

"Time's up Fury, Cross," a guard near the wall announces.

We all stand from the table, shaking hands as Deacon and Rubin prepare to leave. Before we start heading back to our cell, though, I motion for the guard to give me one more moment and wave my uncle over to me.

"I'm sorry," I tell him. "For not being out there for you. I wish I could say I would have done things differently if I had known you were sick, but that would be a lie. You hang on until I get cut loose, you hear me? Don't you putter off while I'm still in here."

"I'm going to try, I promise you that," Deacon says as he gives me one more hug. "It's good having Torin back home helping out. I'm gonna work with him to get him up to speed on all the club business. No matter what happens, I want you to know I'm at peace. Knowing that you and Torin, and now men like that Abe fellow are going to inherit what I've helped build...well, it's all I've ever wanted. I love you, boy. Now get on, before that guard decides to drag me back to the cell with you."

"I love you too, Deacon. We'll take good care of the Savage Kings, I swear to you. No matter where you ride, you can believe that your legacy will always be a group you can be proud of. Take care of your-self, until next time."

"You too, Chase," he says with a smile. "No matter how bad things get, just remember that all of this here is only temporary. The best is yet to come for you, boy. I can feel it in my bones. You may have a long road ahead of you, but you're a Savage fucking King. Don't you ever forget it."

THE END

ALSO BY LANE HART AND D.B. WEST

Catch up with all of the Savage Kings on Amazon:
mybook.to/SavageKingsMC

COMING SOON

Look for Reece's book in March!

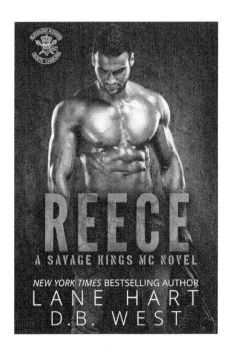

We're also planning books for Miles, Cooper, Sax and Cedric!

ABOUT THE AUTHORS

New York Times bestselling author Lane Hart and husband D.B. West were both born and raised in North Carolina. They still live in the south with their two daughters and enjoy spending the summers on the beach and watching football in the fall.

Connect with D.B.:
Twitter: https://twitter.com/AuthorDBWest
Facebook: https://www.facebook.com/authordbwest/
Website: http://www.dbwestbooks.com
Email: dbwestauthor@outlook.com

Connect with Lane:
Twitter: https://twitter.com/WritingfromHart
Facebook: http://www.facebook.com/lanehartbooks
Instagram: https://www.instagram.com/authorlanehart/
Website: http://www.lanehartbooks.com
Email: lane.hart@hotmail.com